The Never Ending Battle

The Never Ending Battle

FROM WHENCE SHE CAME

Sabrina McDonald

Copyright © 2018 by Sabrina McDonald.

Library of Congress Control Number:		2018902596
ISBN:	Hardcover	978-1-9845-1138-6
	Softcover	978-1-9845-1137-9
	eBook	978-1-9845-1136-2

All rights reserved. No part of this book may be reproduced or transmitted in any form or by any means, electronic or mechanical, including photocopying, recording, or by any information storage and retrieval system, without permission in writing from the copyright owner.

This is a work of fiction. Names, characters, places and incidents either are the product of the author's imagination or are used fictitiously, and any resemblance to any actual persons, living or dead, events, or locales is entirely coincidental.

Any people depicted in stock imagery provided by Getty Images are models, and such images are being used for illustrative purposes only.
Certain stock imagery © Getty Images.

Print information available on the last page.

Rev. date: 02/23/2018

To order additional copies of this book, contact:
Xlibris
1-888-795-4274
www.Xlibris.com
Orders@Xlibris.com
775402

Prologue

"Welcome to history class, my name is Mrs. Sar-" The old woman cut off as chatter resumed as if she wasn't even there. Irritation flitted across her worn face, and she snapped, "Now, really you guys. Pay attention!"

She clapped her hands twice, and the young teens stopped talking, eying the old woman with uncertainty. She was a new teacher, and they had already started making bets on how long she would last. The more generous gave her until the end of the week, the less gave her ten minutes. The class was full of different creatures- from were-animals, to faeries, to trolls.

"And why should we?" sneered one of the boys towards the back, and the rest of the class snickered and guffawed.

"My name is Mrs Sarza, and you will pay attention because-" however, just what reason Mrs. Sarza would give, we will never know. The teens had started conversing with each other again.

"Oh for goodness sake!" growled the old woman, silencing the class yet again, "I have crossed mountains, fought my way through haunted forests, escaped from a cursed town, rescued my sister, and ruled lands and yet," she hissed to the now deathly quiet class, "I have *never* been so disregarded, and so insulted in my life!"

"Y-you ruled a land?" a pretty brunette asked. She had orange eyes, and colorful scales on her arms, legs, and a good portion of her neck, back and chest.

"Lands darlin', *lands*. Oh, how I miss the days," Mrs. Sarza's eyes glazed over, and a smile played at her lips as she recounted many memories in mere seconds. "I remember when it all started, man I was so clueless. Thrown into a world that I had no chance of surviving, and yet here I am."

The old woman sighed, her silvery hair swishing as her shoulders moved with a chuckle. She shook her head, and turned to the white board, apparently ready to start the class, now that she had the student's attention.

However, the students had another idea of how to spend the class, as they urged her to continue.

"You can't stop there-"

"You were just getting to the good part-"

"Oh! You must be Queen Zandriah!"

"Please don't stop!"

Mrs. Sarza turned back around with a grace more fitting for a woman in her thirties, not one well into her nineties. "Now, now children. First, Zandriah is my sister, I am Avalon, and I will strike a deal with you. Consider it a bargain."

The children looked at the old woman with a new found respect. They had grown up with stories about Avalon, but none of them have ever thought that they would actually meet the woman know as The Queen- the woman who saved their world quite by accident.

"Can you tell us the story-" a scrawny, wide-eyed boy started to ask, but trailed away as soon as the other teens hissed at him.

"Can I tell you the story of what?" Mrs. Sarza asked, her eyes twinkling with kindness and a firmness that told everyone else to be respectful.

"The story of Bane?" The boy finished, and then sunk in his chair, as if talking had taken all of his energy. He tugged his hood over his long blond hair, and folded his arms over his chest. He was the only human besides the teacher, and many of the magical creatures didn't like him for it.

"Ah, yes. Well, I can tell you about our first encounter, but I'm afraid I just don't have time for the whole story today. Which brings me back to my deal. If you all can behave, then I will tell you all about my adventures throughout the school year."

The deal was quickly agreed to, and everybody seemed to hold their breath, as the old woman began her story. Her eyes went slightly dark, and you could hear poorly concealed bitterness in her voice.

"The day my mother died is bore into my head. The last thing that dared to cross my mothers' lips was the worst sound ever heard, and if you heard it you would agree, it was the scream of defeat and agony, and it will haunt me forever, until death."

Chapter 1

I stepped out into the warm summer air. The sun was rapidly descending behind the mountains, but the air remained soothingly warm. Spring had been savage, more like a second winter rather than spring. Now there were no signs of snow, and even the last bit of frost had disappeared. Fog could be seen in the distance, mingling with the white tipped mountains. Taking a deep breath, I walked to the middle of the back yard. The ankle high grass tickled my bare feet, and a smile stole across my face. Even a month after the end of the deep freeze, it still sent shivers of pleasure down my spine to see the thriving wild blackberry bushes, and my abundant garden growing with every passing day. I ran my fingers through my short bluish-black hair. My mom had just cut it the day before because the heat made my thick hair frizz and my neck become slick with sweat the moment I would walk out the door. It was now an inch long, and easier to style than waking up in the morning. My sister had scoffed, saying that girls shouldn't have short hair, and that she would never have her long, chestnut brown hair shorter than shoulder length. Despite our differences, my sister and I were the best of friends. Besides, she was always the athletic one. She would hunt, and I would garden, so I guess you could say that we were even on our "boyish ways" as she would put it.

"Avalon," My mother called from the back door, "It's time for dinner!" Then she disappeared.

I sighed and headed into the house. Today was a special day. My garden had finally produced edible fruits and vegetables. On top of that, my sister, Zandriah had had an amazing hunt the day before.

I headed back into the house, and closed the door. As I passed the mirror on the wall, I stopped and obsessed over my looks for the millionth time. My now short, more blue than black hair spiked up naturally in all directions.It suited my personality quite well, and looked much better on me than long hair, or even chin length hair. Short, spiky hair suited my dad as well. My skin was deathly pale, and easily bruised. My eyes were a bright, almost unnaturally toxic looking, green with flecks of silver. Just like him. My build was small and fragile looking, yet my muscles had been worked until they became hard and unyielding. Not that you would be able to tell that just by looking at me. Not quite short, and yet not tall, I stood at five foot six...and a half. He had been the same.

I fingered the little diamond at my throat as I let my thoughts wonder back to the day I was six years old. My sister was five at the time, and we were unable to completely grasp what was going on. Back then, 'passed away' meant that he was away, but would come back as time passed. If only we had known.

My sister has no idea how lucky she is I thought bitterly. She didn't see dad every time she looked at herself in the mirror. Instead she saw a mixture of mom and dad. She had mom's chestnut brown hair and dad's pale skin. Although, hers wasn't quite as pale as mine and dad's. Her eyes were indeed green, yet they were a beautiful dark green with flecks of dark gray, and bright gold. She was five feet four inches flat, a mere half inch taller than mom.

Mom had long chestnut brown hair, blue eyes, and not quite pale skin. She was a cheery woman with a forever optimistic look on life. Sometimes it got quite annoying, and other times it was just what we needed. Zandriah got her personality from mom. I have no idea where my 'hide from the world and hope that nobody notices me' personality came from. Maybe dad was an introvert.

"Avalon," mom sang from the kitchen.

"On my way," I hollered back. I sighed and made my way to the dining room table. The feast looked amazing. A grouse with a sweet sauce and an assortment of vegetables. Candles were lit all over, and the fire was blazing in the living room. One of my favorite parts of our little house was the lack of walls between the kitchen, dining room, and living room. The kitchen and the living room were right next to each other, and the living room stretched the length of both of them. Although, that wasn't saying much because the house was so small.

We all sat down, thanked the Lord and Lady for the meal, and began to eat. For the first couple of minutes the only sounds that could be heard was that of dishing up and digging in.

"This grouse is so delicious, Zandriah. I will never be as good as you with a bow and arrow," I told my little sister as I shoved more food into my mouth. Zandriah blushed crimson. Mom nodded her head in agreement as she washed down a particularly large mouthful of food with a swig of blackberry juice.

"These sweet potatoes are amazing, and this blackberry juice is great," Zandriah countered, "It has just the right amount of tartness to offset the sweetness. Plus, my hunting wouldn't do us any good if mom wasn't here to cook it."

"Oh, and thank you, Avalon, you were right about the mint, it mixes perfectly with the grouse. I don't know what we would do without your garden," mom managed to say in between bites. We were all in high spirits, and we were doing our best not to start a fight. It was the first time all year that we have had full stomachs, and there was no point in spoiling all the good with a petty fight, besides we all love each other and end up forgiving each other within hours anyway.

My sister had shot half a dozen plump grouse and a wild hare yesterday, so we had spent the day plucking and skinning in joy. Then we prepared one grouse for cooking, and put the rest in the freezer. It took all day to prep the grouse. The next day I had raided my garden, finding the perfect sweet potatoes, and picking the ripest blackberries, which grew on the edge of the seemingly endless forest. I had sorted through my mint, and plucked the freshest leaves. To finish it off, I picked an assortment of vegetables to have on the side.

Deep in the forest grew some more blackberries. These were better, but were about an hour away, and I didn't want to wait that long for dinner. The clearing where the blackberries grew was huge, and it was always full of wildlife. Only Zandriah and I have been there. There is an apple tree at the edge of the clearing, and we climb it to grab the best apples. We grab about a dozen, and we feed them to the wildlife. Sometimes we eat one too, but we usually just feed the animals.

In our clearing, we lay near the deer and the wild hares, and we watch the sun set as the moon rises to cast a lovely shadow over everything. It has always been easy for my sister and I to befriend animals. We do our own thing, and leave them alone. It seems to make them curious more than wary. Sometimes, if we are quiet and calm enough, we are able to pet them for a bit. It is a beautiful moment when an animal trusts you enough to let you pet them, let alone a wild animal.

"Do you guys mind if I take some of this dinner to your grandmother," my mom asked cautiously, snapping me out of my thought. If mom brought this meal to grandmother, she'd be gone for about a week, because grams lived a day away by car, and all we own is a horse. Zandriah groaned. She hated it when mom left, it always left her in a state of mild panic until mom came back as safe and sound as she left.

"Sure, mom," I said loudly, kicking Zandriah under the table, "we'll be okay."

Zandriah frowned, and rubbed her shin as mom and I chuckled. Zandriah stuck her tongue out at me and made a face, which made mom and I laugh. She chortled, and rolled her eyes as if we were the ones being childish.

The laughing died down, and we finished our dinner with an air of tranquility. After everybody was stuffed, we started to pack up the leftovers, and put our dishes away. Zandriah put her plate in the sink, and it made an unusually loud crash. Only, it couldn't have been her plate, because it was too loud, and sounded as if it was coming from far away outside. To put on top of that, it sounded more like a bang than a crash. We all froze, and looked toward the front door. Zandriah and I shook our heads and chuckled together, but mom seemed nervous. Borderline scared. My sister and I looked at each other quizically, as if we were sharing some sort of inside joke. After all, it wasn't the first time mom has gotten scared over the backfire of an old truck, or the falling of an old, dead tree.

Mom rushed out of the kitchen and into her room, as silent and swiftly as if she was floating. My sister and I stood rooted to where we were at the time of the loud crash. Surely she was just being dramatic? Nevertheless, she came back into the kitchen with two backpacks.

They were the survival packs that we had made when we were very young. I doubt Zandriah even really remembers it. I hardly did. Mom handed one to me, and the other to a bewildered Zandriah. She looked all around, as if she was expecting somebody to barge into the room any second. I felt something dark grip my soul. My heartbeat sped up, and my hands started to shake slightly.

"Mom?" I whispered, moving at long last. I cupped my moms face in my hands. I saw tears streaking down her face, "What's wrong? You're scaring me."

Mom took a deep breath, and I studied her as she steeled herself from some truth that she was hiding from her daughters. Zandriah cleared her throat, and made a jerky movement as another loud bang was heard, this time closer. Mom looked at the front door, and when she turned back to me, there was unmistakable fear on her face, and tears in her eyes. However, when she spoke her voice was expressionless and steady.

"You need to listen to me very carefully," I gripped the straps of my backpack tighter as she spoke, "your lives depend on it."

"Mom," I laughed nervously, "is this some sort of joke? I'm sure the noises were just some vehicle backfiring. I swear, you are always jumping at the slightest--"

"*Listen*" mom hissed, and I fell silent. She pulled out a pad and paper from one of the kitchen drawers, and wrote furiously as she spoke, "You need to get to the desert to the North. To get there you must go through the forest at the back of our house. Once through, you'll need to go over the mountains. There are too many sharp rocks at the base to go through them, and you can't go around them because there is a river on one side, and the forest gets too thick on the other. Always head North. In the middle of the mountains, there is a town. If you come across it, *don't go in! You must go around!*" she stopped briefly to look back, but I didn't dare interrupt her. Even though it all sounded so crazy, and I was half expecting her to tell me this was all a joke. A part of me was also half expecting somebody to barge through the door and kill us or a bomb to be dropped on our house or something. Mom turned back to us as another loud bang, very close this time, sounded outside. She took a deep breath and continued, "Don't go into the town, they play nasty tricks, one is that they make it look like it's abandoned, but it is not. You must go around it. Next, you'll come to a huge forest. Trees as tall as mansions with trunks as big as semi trucks. Stick to the path, and if you come to a fork, go North. At the end of that forest, you'll come to a desert. Say 'honestum appareo'."

"honest appareo," I repeated.

"honest*rum* appario" mom repeated, a little exasperated.

"Sorry," I muttered, "honestrum appareo."

"Good. Now, make sure that you don't stop to talk to anybody."

"What if-" My sister began.

"No!" Mom growled, and my sister closed her mouth, "You mustn't stop. Go out the back door, and I'll keep them distracted."

"Who? What is going on, mom?" I asked. My sister was inching toward the back door, but I wanted answers. Now.

"There's no time! You need to go," mom grabbed my wrist and pulled me to toward the back door. We were about halfway there when we heard footsteps from the front deck. Zandriah and I rushed out the back door, and mom rushed toward the front door. I wanted with all my heart to pull her with me, but something inside me told me to get my sister out safe. So I listened, and grabbed her arm before she could fling the door open. I cracked the door open, and squeezed out quietly, and motioned for my sister to follow. After we were both outside, she slowly closed the door, and we stood there looking at the forest, letting our eyes adjust, and wondering if it was safe to move out of the shadows.

"Come on," I whispered barely audible, making up my mind. I shifted my bag more securely on my back, and Zandriah followed suit. She went to go walk out of the shadows as another loud bang sounded, and I grabbed my sister and jerked her against the house. A bullet whistled by our heads. I let go of her hand, and took a deep breathe. A tear roll down my eye. The man probably thought he saw an animal, they had to have encountered a few on the way here. The bangs we had heard were undoubtedly from the men killing wildlife that crossed their path. The man grunted, and turned around, looking around the corner of the house. Summoning our courage, we gathered ourselves to sprint across the dark yard. We had barely moved an inch when we heard a female voice slice through the quiet tension of the house, making it explode with unyielding fury.

"Darek!" it screamed, "Get in here! She won't stop squirming, and somebody find those brats, now!"

My sister and I shot out of the shadows of the house as soon as he disappeared, and bolted towards the forest. Bullets whizzed by us, and many near misses had my heart beating faster and faster. I grabbed Zandriah's hand to make sure that she was still there, and continued to run. Just as we reached the edge of the forest, I felt her drop like a weight. I couldn't figure out who was shooting at us. I looked back to see if I could catch a glimpse of where the shooter was, and saw a familiar man's face. *Dad.* Shock coursed through me, but I knew it wasn't him. It couldn't be, he was dead. Mom said so.

Frantically looking for a spot to hide, I grabbed my sister's hand just to make sure that she was still there. I spotted a cluster of boulders, and pulled her with me to hide behind them. Her pained yelp didn't quite register in my mind as I continued to drag her toward what I considered a few seconds of safety. Maybe there we could stop and think about our next step. How were we going to get away from our pursuers?

My thoughts were interuppted by the sound of shattering glass. I peeked around the tree that I was hiding behind. Somebody had thrown a lit torch through a window, and the flames were consuming the house at a steady pace. There was about a dozen men outside, two of which were holding our mom hostage. Her hands were tied behind her back, and she was on her knees facing the house.

One of the men bent over and said something to her. It must've been horrible, because she screamed in agony, and thrashed wildly about. Zandriah and I turned to run deeper into the forest. It would only be a matter of time before they started to hunt us down. I froze at the sound of a distant gunshot. Zandriah stumbled a few more paces, then stopped as well. I had no way of knowing whether or not she had heard the gunshot.

"Avalon," my sister whimpered, but I ignored her. I was trying to hide my grief, and work in my mind the best course of action at the same time. She repeated my name with more urgency. I looked down at her, and saw blood leaking from her left forearm. Not a whole lot, yet I started to panic, and my hands immediately started to shake. I knelt beside her to try and stop the bleeding. My mind shut down, and I started crying furiously, so trying to find the right bandages in my backpack seemed near impossible. Finally, I found a sterile white pad and some athletic tape. I ripped open the package, and gingerly placed the pad on her arm. I grabbed the tape, and rolled it around her arm several times before realizing that I hadn't peeled it, so nothing was happening. I let out a snort of frustration as I peeled the tape. Placing the sticky side on the bandage, I started to roll the tape around her arm again, this time leaving a trail that will keep the bandage on without cutting circulation. Hopefully. The job was sloppy, but it held, and I knew that it would have to do for now. I bent down, and ripped off the extra tape with my teeth.

I helped her up and steadied her. She seemed a little light headed, but there was no time to lose, the sounds of yelling were getting louder. Hand in hand, we left at a stumbling jog. I had no idea where we were going, or where our destination was, I knew that mom wanted us to go to some mountains, but how were we supposed to know where they were? It's not like we had a map, or time to look at a map to see where the hell we were going. Not even a compass could be found in the backpack, although I could've sworn we put them in there somewhere.

Zandriah and I stumbled over rocks and roots that poked out of the ground. I looked around, but everything looked so confusing. I had been in this forest thousands of times, but it all seemed so different now, so alien. I could tell that my sister was having trouble keeping up, but we had to keep moving. I took random lefts and rights, and Zandriah followed me, putting her trust in me to keep her alive. The fear that I hadn't allowed myself to feel before rose in my throat without warning, and made me want to throw up. It had given me no time to fight it away, and my emotional strength was slipping away like water through my fingers. I stopped in my tracks as if I had just hit a brick wall. My vision went blurry as I bent over, starting to hyperventilate. I gasped for breath, felt a burning in my throat, and tried to fight the urge to be ill. Dropping to my hands and knees, I heaved, but nothing came up.

"Avalon?" my sister's panicked voice seemed distorted and far away, "Avalon? We have to go, they're coming."

I tried to regain balance and a straight posture, but only managed to topple over, and rest on my back. My vision slowly came back to me as I laid there, blinking rapidly.

"Avalon," I heard my sister scream. My senses snapped back, and I sat up just in time to see a small group of men running at us full speed. I took a deep breath, pushed all thought of a mental breakdown out of my head, and stood up. Zandriah grabbed my hand, turned, and fled with me in tow. We crashed through the woods, and stumbled over roots. The forest seemed to come alive below our feet. Throwing its roots out at us, hitting us with low hanging tree branches, and throwing noisy dry leaves on the ground. It was like a game where the forest ensured that we were not going to be able to slip away quietly. If we won, we survived, if we didn't...

"Hurry up men!" The female voice from before screeched. I looked back quickly, and saw a woman among the men about twenty feet away. She had what looked like navy blue hair, but it was hard to tell in the dark forest. She was thin, and average height. As I looked into her eyes I stumbled. With metallic purples, silvers, and blues, her eyes were entrancing. It looked as if somebody had taken her eyes out of their sockets, dipped them in oil for a few hours, and put them back to dry. My own green eyes widened, and while a part of me was repulsed by the woman's eyes, another part of me was fascinated by them, and wanted to surrender to them. They were so beautiful, yet disturbing.

As I slowed, Zandriah remained oblivious, which caused her to keep pace, and jerk me back into reality. I shook my head of all thoughts except for one; survive. We raced through the forest yet again, and the ground that we had lost when I was assessing the enemy, was gained again and then some. Within ten minutes, we were so far ahead that we could no longer hear or see them. We didn't stop though, instead, we ran until our sides hurt, then we ran until the pain was unbearable. After that we slowed to a jog, and then to a walk until we could jog again. About four hours after losing sight of the men and woman, my legs gave out from under me.

"S-stop. I c-can't. Go….On." I gasped. Flushed faces, sticky with sweat, heaving gasps of breath, and feeling as if the running had brought death himself to our door, we laid on our backs, watching the dying sun through the treetops. I crawled to the root of a tree, and heaved once again, this time giving into the urge of being ill. I shook and cried in grief and pain, with no intentions of attempting to keep quiet. A little ways off, I knew Zandriah was sitting in silence. She was never one to show her emotions, she preferred to bottle them up inside instead, claiming that it made her strong.

After a few minutes, I dried my eyes, took a deep breath, and wiped my mouth clean with an alcohol wipe from my first aid backpack. A short rummage through the packs produced snack bars for both of us, two water bottles, and in the side pockets, two compasses. We decided to save the snack bars for more desperate times, and drank a little water from one bottle. Everything except for the compasses found their way back into the bag. I struggled to my feet, and Zandriah followed suit.

"North is that way" I said, pointing to the left. "We can head that way tomorrow, but there's no point in going that way now. It'll be completely dark soon, and we'll get lost. Better to just find shelter."

Looking around, we found a patch of ferns nearby. There were a couple boulders behind them, and the fantasy that there was some sort of small deer den played in my head. Completely illogical, of course. Nevertheless, the ferns would offer a little hideout. We decided to go through the small gap between the boulders and the ferns so that we wouldn't destroy any of the ferns. It was a tight squeeze to get in without making it obvious somebody had taken shelter. Then, we had to replace some of the leaves of the fern plants carefully so that it looked undisturbed, because even the slightest hint could send them our way. Turning around, I saw that there was no den, but instead a wide clearing. The boulders made walls, and once inside, we noticed that instead of two, there were eight boulders, placed oddly against each other by mother nature. We could only army crawl around because the walls weren't that high, and if we stood up, the tops of our heads might be seen. However, we were only there to sleep, so that was okay. We got into semi-comfortable positions, and we were fast asleep within seconds.

My dreams were scattered, causing me to toss and turn all night. I couldn't even stay asleep; dreams of the past wouldn't let me. All the good times, and the bad. Dreams of fights, and joy. Of disagreements, and agreements. How we used to play and joke, and just plain live.

When I woke that morning, I hoped with every aching bone in my body that it was all just a big nightmare. I opened one eye, then the other, and snapped them shut at the sight of ferns and dirt. I repeated my actions slowly, without closing my eyes, and groaned. I scanned for my sister and found her a little ways off to my right, curled in a little ball.

I pulled my body towards her, gritting my teeth against the horrid pain that shot up my legs, stabbed at my arms, and pitted in my stomach. Knowing that she was in just as much pain as me, I very gently shook her awake.

"Zandriah, sweetheart, time to get up." I whispered in her ear, "It's almost sunrise, come on, get up!" I coaxed her sweetly, my voice cracking. The more I looked at her, the more I noticed how much she resembled mom. From her chestnut brown hair, to the way she slightly smiled in her sleep, as if she were telling a funny joke. Mom used to do that all the time. Then I thought about my bright green eyes, my skin that was a couple shades lighter than theirs, and my dark bluish black hair...like my dad. I shook her gently again, rougher than I had intended.

"I'm up, just please don't touch me, it hurts too much. God, that dream felt so... Real." she whimpered, barely audible. She started to move, and then stopped as the pain flashed in her eyes. She looked around, and tried, unsuccessfully, to bite back a terrified sob.

She swallowed and whispered, "So it's not a dream, its real? It's all..." her voice trailed. Then she did something so out of character, so wild, that I jumped back, and looked at her in horror. Zandriah wailed.

"No, *no!* Not mom! *No, no, no*! I won't believe it, take me home, take me home now! She's still alive!" She screamed. It was plain to see that she wasn't convincing herself.

Tears welled up in her eyes as we stood and made our way through the knee high ferns, not bothering with keeping the surroundings pristine. We got out, and I pulled her close, even though it hurt every bone in my seemingly broken body. A single tear fell from my eyes as I made a silent vow. I would, from now on, stay strong for my sister, this would be the last tear, and they would pay. Whoever did this to my mom, to my sister, and to me, would pay. I slowly, painfully, bent down and picked up our packs.

A sound was heard from the forest. Somebody had stepped on a twig, and alerted every living creature in the surrounding area that they were there.

Pain would have to overome us on another day, because there was no time for it now. We ran on strained and cramping muscles away from the familiar female voice in the distance. "I can see them, don't let them get away, we need those necklaces! *Hurry! Now!*"

Weaving in and out of trees, jumping over stumps, we sprinted away from the murderers. Turning my head, I could see that they were slowly gaining on us. They would catch us within the hour, I just knew it.

"No, majesty, they are but deer, not the girls! Your eyes have lied to you!" there was no feeling in the man's commanding voice, but it seemed to have stopped the chase for a short time. We of course, kept going, trying to get some distance between us and them. We knew they would continue to look, and they would find us if we didn't keep moving.

The man's words were ringing in my ears as we approached the foot of the mountain. He sounded so much like my father had, and yet it couldn't be. My mind went back to what he had said. It was odd. His flat voice. The way he worded his sentence. Even what he called her. *Majesty*. As if she owned him, as if he was a servant. As if....as if he lived for her, and she was his one and only family. Maybe he really did believe that we were nothing but a pair of scrawny, graceful, meaty flesh with antlers and hooves.

Less than ten minutes later, we burst out of the trees to find our next struggle. Mountains that seemed as high as the sky itself towered supreme. It seemed that instead of touching level ground, kissing mountains just made a small divit. No matter how you looked at it, we would have to climb. Luckily, we were able to find a place where two mountains met within minutes.

"Maybe it really would be better to just find a way around," My sisters' hesitant voice bounced around what seemed to be my head. However, it was all so distant, so unreal. I was almost convinced it was all just a nightmare. Almost. Something seemed missing, seemed out of place. Could it really be him? It was a tentitive, frivolous hope. Not very probable either. The father that I remembered was happy. He would never help he people who would want to hurt his wife and kids, even if he hadn't seen them in years.

"Come on, let's go!" I snapped as I came out of my trance-like state. "We need to go before they find out he was lying!" I swallowed the lump in my throat, and started to climb.

"I-I can't, I am a-afraid o-of...of-" Zandriah's voice trailed off, and her face grew pink in her discomfort.

"Do not tell me you are afraid of heights at a time like this, now climb!" my patience and sanity were running dangerously low. I jumped down in frustration and shoved her up the base of the mountain. After a couple steps, Zandriah finally gave up and started to climb.

"I see' em! They're climbing over the mountains!" the husky voice insulted my ears and sent a shiver down my back so violent; it nearly sent me over the edge. The voice was getting closer as we climbed. "Hurry up men; we're closing in on them!"

Crap. How are we supposed to get away from them now? "Climb faster! Climb until you can't climb anymore! Hurry!" I yelled up to my sister as they neared. I took a brief second to look at my watch, which read 9:00 AM, and took a mental note of how long we would have until the sun went down...Summer nights are long, so the light will stay until about 9PM. Twelve hours.

We were lucky enough to find a gap in the mountains, right off the bat. With relitively high energy, some water that would normally last us about half a day, and our hopes higher than the tops of the mountains, we embarked on our newest challenge with vigour. Our first mountain climb took two hours of steady climbing to get to the top, and one and a half hours to get to the bottom. We realized a little late that a slow pace is preffered when climbing, especially when clumsiness and inexperience come in to play. By the time we reached the bottom of the first mountain climb, it was almost one in the afternoon.

"Eat this," I said, and passed one of the snack bars over to Zandriah. We ate slowly, trying to avoid upset stomachs. Not that our stomachs could get much more upset. they were yelling and clawing with hunger.

"We only have eight each, so we should eat one tonight, and two in the morning," Zandria said. I nodded my head. This was going to be quiet difficult. Had we been in better shape, the climb would've been faster and easier. However, food was scarse, our water supply was dangerously low, and our muscles were prone to cramping. It was a miracle we could climb at all.

We looked up at a large mountain, and shared a groan. One hand over the other. One foot placed so it could vault the body up on to a walkable ledge. Pull with the arms, push with the legs. Was this proper form? How the hell should I know? I've never climbed anything bigger than a ladder before. The climb itself was uneventful. there was no sign of anybody or anything other than us and the mountains. This was relieving and disconcerting at the same time. If they weren't here, then where were they? Maybe they are just hiding, waiting for the right time to pounce.

A little after eight thirty, we found ourselves at the bottom of the mountain, and facing another big mountain. We decided the climbing all the way over took longer because even though we were able to hug the mountain and cautiously climb up as if we were on a small hill, it took longer, and was more exhausting at the end of the day. Besides, there were more small caves to rest in when we took the in betweens.

Nine O'Clock came around, and the realization that we had climbed and walked and busted our asses for twelve hours dawnd on us. Moo wonder we felt so dead. We climbed up an in between for twenty minutes, and stopped at the first cave we came to.

"Let's stretch. maybe we'll feel better," I croaked. My throat was dry because we hadn't had any water to drink since two in the afternoon, and my stomach rumbled in hunger. We sat down, and stretched for fifteen minutes. It felt so good to stretch out aching, strained muscles.

Food was handed out, and we ended up eating three bars each. Instant regret hit us as our thirst multiplied, and our rations depleted. We knew that we had to find water tomorrow, or we would die of dehydration, but that is tomorrow's problem. I pulled my compass out of my pocket, and checked to see if it still worked. It had stayed in my pocket all day, and I had felt it hit the mountain more than a few times during the climb. It looked fine, so I stored it back in my pocket, and laid my pack down in the far corner of the cave. Both Zandriah and I knew that we would have to get up early to make sure we were out before anybody could find us.

"My watch is set for five in the morning," I said. The response was a grunt, and I took it as a confirmation of Zandriah hearing me. I laid my head on the pillow, and gave in to exhaustion.

Chapter 2

Panic. Fear. Undeniable frustration. All of this, and more, was running through my veins, heightening my senses, and driving my mind and body crazy. On the plus side, it also made me numb to any pain that came my way. Zandriah and I were climbing as fast as we could, trying to get away from the beasts that were hunting us as light started to shine over the mountain top. We had no clue who, or what, they were. We only knew we were being hunted by snarling, growling, fast, vicious beasts… and that we forgot our survival packs back where we slept, leaving us with nothing to defend ourselves with. Our knives were in there. Not to mention food. However, it was too late to go back, and there were more important things to concentrate on, like avoiding being eaten.

We had no clue how many there were, or what they were… Until I slipped, and started to fall. I clawed for a hold, anything that could save me from the unforgiving death that was sure to come with the jagged rocks that made up the mountainside. The thought, oddly, made my fear vanish, and with it, all my hope. As I stopped clawing, and just waited for death, waited for the black to consume me, all I could think was, *I let her down, I let my mom down! How could I?* However, as I fell, two seconds felt like two hours, and the wait was unbearable. I started to claw in vain again.

Then, the sensation of falling ceased abrubtly. At first, I thought that maybe I had just become numb to that feeling too, but then I realized that something had snatched my shirt. Now all I could think was that Zandriah came to save me. I looked up to thank her, and stifled a scream at what met my eyes. It was not Zandriah at all. Above me stood a big, terrifying white tiger. It was pulling me up by the scruff of my shirt as she might a kit by the scruff of the neck. Tenderly, as if I were to die at any given moment. Which I would've if he (she? It?) Didn't come at that very second. The longer I looked into those eyes, the more I saw. It was not unkindness I saw, no. a little wild, yes, but not vicious, demanding, or hungry. If I didn't know better, I'd say it was motherly. Our eyes stayed locked as she pulled me up, and then it hit me, this was them, the guardians mom told us about.

"Avalon!" Zandriah was scaling down the mountainside when I was just getting past the point of sheer terror, and into shock. "No! Grab my hand! Before it hurts you!" Terror brimmed my sisters' voice, and snapped me back to the present.

"Stop, Zandriah, don't come any closer," I told her calmly. She stopped, disbelief etched across her face.

"Wh-What do you mean?" Her voice and eyes were overflowing with fearful tears. "Come on Avalon!" she begged. "Please, sis, I can't go on without you! Back up slowly, and, and, we can get out of here. Stop looking it in the eyes. Avalon! Lets go, before they eat us!"

"I don't think they'll eat us, Zandriah." I reassured her as she started to cry. "Zandriah, they won't hurt us."

"But they are wild, vicious beasts!" She was beside herself.

"This all seems so familiar, but I can't remember it's like a dream or a story or, *something!*" I said in frustration, ignoring her. Zandriah looked at the white tiger closest to her. Her eyes slowly brightened with curiosity and almost all fear was gone when she saw what I had seen long before. Then….

"Avalon, I know this might sound crazy but, well, what if…." Zandriah hesitated long enough for me to get nervous.

"But what, Zandriah, but what!" I almost screamed, and would have, if it weren't for my fear of disturbing the great beasts that stared at us as if to say, *'Are you guys crazy? Let's go!'*

Zandriah took in a deep breath before she spoke, "Do you remember mom's story? About the great beasts? The ones who traveled the world in search of the lost souls who bear the two necklaces of power and honor?"

"Yeah, why?" I asked, not letting my eyes leave the white tiger in front of me. Then I understood what she was getting at, "No. We are not in some whacked out story our mom used to tell us, so just forget it! Anyway, we have three necklaces, not two." I decided it was time to take a risk, and turned to walk down the mountainside.

"Where are you going? It is way too early to go anywhere! And aren't we supposed to be going up, not down?" Zandriah asked.

"We need our stuff, unless you want to hunt up food and water. Also, we need to get going anyway, the sun is rising," I snapped back at her. She started to follow me, though she looked immensely offended. We hadn't taken more than four steps when we heard a warning growl from one of the white tigers, and a rustling in the bushes.

"Run!" I yelled. We both turned and ran up the mountainside with the beasts by our sides as a figure jumped out of the bushes and tried to grasp onto my sister. He succeeded. The force of his yank sent Zandriah sprawling, and he lost his hold on her. Luckily I was there to catch her, steady her, turn, and keep moving.

Within minutes, there were so many people, it was like red ants on an anthill chasing four intruding, defenseless, black ants. We ran up the mountainside, hoping we could cheat certain death once again, hoping that we could out run them. We got to the peak of the mountain, and started to skid down the side without hesitating. We both lost our footing a time or two, but we got back our balance.

Then, a voice spoke out to me, as if it was in my head, but then again not quite. I could hear it plain as day when it told me to swerve right, but I could've sworn it was in my head. However, I did swerve to my right, and so did the other three. Then I went with the voice inside my head and went back down, then to the left, then down. Then another left, down, right, and so on.

I noticed that the path we were taking seemed to be full of weird brush that gave us a bit of cover, yet didn't slow our pace. Our descent was twice as fast as our ascent, and infinitely more terrifying. Had the desire struck, there was no way to stop quickly. Not that we really wanted to, because even though we were quite a ways ahead of the army, they were *an army*, and we were four defenseless black ants. Our pace started to slow rapidly after a couple hours. It took a few minutes, but we were eventually stumbling down at what would've been a walk, had we been on flat ground. We were resting at a cave when I realized that the voices had faded a long time ago, and that we were going to camp here for a while.

"It was like you were reading my mind Avalon!" Zandriah smiled excitedly, "Whenever I thought left, you went left! It was weird, though," Zandriah frowned, "It was almost as if *I* wasn't thinking them, but hearing them, really. Well, not really hearing them either, but... I don't really know, it's hard to explain."

I just grunted. I wasn't in the mood to talk, and I was in too much pain to do so anyway, so I didn't say anything. My sides felt like they were being torn open by the beasts, and I could feel cramps start to form (not for the first time on this journey) in both my legs. Zandriah talked about making a fire, but decided against it when I sent her a 'do you want to be killed' look. Then, she and I snuggled against each other, and the white tigers laid next to us, I assumed to give us heat and a sense of security that we haven't had since we've left home. For the first time in what seems like ages, I slept soundly through the night, and woke up refreshed, and oddly only a little sore. As our journey continued, we talked about the voices.

"I haven't heard them since yesterday," I admitted.

"Me either, I wonder where they came from?"

"Beats me."

We were whispering as we crept down the mountain in the cover of shrubs, and large boulders that threatened to topple over the side of the mountain. It made the decent a little slower, but we were almost to the bottom, so I didn't mind so much. Besides, there were men and women scouring the mountain,, turning it upside down, looking for us. I could hear them in the distance, marching, yelling, and getting closer.

"Are we going to die?" The question caught me off guard. My sister was looking at me intensely, waiting for a flicker of fear or admission of defeat. I kept my face carefully blank as I thought about my response. It was quite difficult, as I had always unashamedly worn my feelings on my face.

"No, We are going to be just fine, and we are going to live to be a hundred years old. We will get all wrinkly and creaky. I will protect you, and we will live through this," I whispered, trying to keep the doubt out of my voice.

"Promise?"

"I promise."

We spent the rest of the day in silence. It went by slow, and it was all that I could do to stop from whooping with joy when we reached a nook near the bottom of the mountain. Settling in close to each other, we gave into unconsciousness. Beyond the point of dreams, we merely slept in order to replenish a small amount of energy that we had lost with every passing moment in the long, arduous days.

Sometime during the night, a shuffling of bodies made me half wake up, and I could've sworn I heard a couple voices say goodbye. Morning came swiftly with an unpleasant discovery for my sister and I. Our companions were gone.

"Come on Zandriah, lets go," I said, as she searched for any sign of the white tigers. I knew that it would be useless. Why else would they leave in the middle of the night? We looked ahead to a town that didn't look deserted in the least. In fact, it was positively swarming with what looked like happy, somewhat underfed, people. I looked over at Zandriah, and she looked back at me with a shrug.

"Maybe this isn't the town that mom was talking about." Zandriah said, and started for the border.

"Zandriah! What do you think you are doing?" I whispered, grabbing her arm. She tugged free with ease, giving me a death glare.

"This is obviously not the town that mom was talking about, and, being as we left our food in our packs and our packs are on the other side of the mountains, I am starving so..." Zandriah kept walking. I quickly followed her, even though I knew it was the worst thing we could do.

Chapter 3

We inched our way to the very border of the town. The people were all smiling, and walking with an extra little hop in their steps. Yet, their smiles seemed strained, their skin was a little grayish, and the hops seemed jerky. Almost pained. Something was off about the town, but Zandriah seemed so sure that everything was okay, and I was always known as the paranoid one (not that that is necessarily always a bad thing.)

Zandriah took a deep breath, boldly stepping into the town. I closed my eyes, and took a half dozen baby steps over the border, before opening one eye. Nothing happened. Nobody noticed us, fire didn't get thrown down from the tops of buildings, there were no angry shouts from monsters. In fact, it was almost as if we were invisible. Zandriah shrugged when I looked over at her. Maybe they just didn't care.

I held out my hand, and my sister took it, giving me a small smile. Heads held high, we made our way to the people that seemed to be gathering in the center of the town. As we got closer to the middle, a few stragglers looked over to us, and my heart stopped. The eyes were wrong. They were red, like a vampire or demon from a horror movie. The pupils were dilated, giving them a sinister hungry look. To put on top of that, their faces seemed to lack any muscle and fat, and instead was just greyish skin melted poorly onto bone. His smile revealed several missing teeth, and his nose drooped like a deflated balloon.

He's a zombie, I thought in shock. Nothing else seemed to fit, but how could it be? Zombies are not real! Too paralyzed to move or talk, I merely tightened the grip on my sister's hand who by now had started screaming in horror. *So much for never showing your emotions, sis* The fleeting thought crossed my mind, and I couldn't help but be momentarily amused at the role reversal her and I have done. That is, until I felt her grip being yanked out of mine.

"Zandriah!" I screamed to her, over and over. I looked left and right. The zombies seemed to multiply. No matter where I looked, all I saw were red eyes and greyish skin. Bony fingers wrapped around my wrist. Sharp fingernails dug into my ankles. Unbelievably strong yet soft arms wrapped around my waist.

"I'm here!" She called back, and I fought my way out of the grip of a dozen hands, making my way towards Zandriah's voice.

I felt an arm grab me from behind, tearing new cuts into my flesh. I yelled in pain, trying to pull free, but only making the damage to my skin worse.

"Zandriah!" I screamed yet again. It was the only thing i could seem to say.

"Avalon!"

Don't let go of my hand, I thought. I tried to yell to her, but the words got stuck in my throat. I tried to yell her name. *Whatever you do, just don't let go...*

Finger bones covered my mouth, leaving more nail marks on my cheeks. As soon as I find mysister and I get wrenched apart by bony hands.

"No!" I heard my sister scream, "No! Avalon!"

I kicked out, squirmed, and thrust my elbows into the bodies around me. I knew that the only hope of getting free was to keep moving, but the more I squirmed, the more the grip on my body seemed tighten. Especially the one around my neck. My vision started to blur, and panic rushed through me. I remembered my mom telling me one time that people flail wildly before they pass out. It is the bodies way of defending itself.

Well, there's only one way to find out if it convinces them. No longer worried with whether or not I was hitting the enemy, I started to contort and flail my limbs wildly as if I had lost control. After a few seconds, I hung limp, playing dead. Arms immediately slackened, the ones around my throat let go completely. Slowly, my body was freed from the grasps of the monsters, and I was left alone on the ground for the time being. Blood rushed to my head, my arms and legs were asleep, but i was free.

"Avalon!" My sister's voice pierced my heart, and it took everything I had to not open my eyes, and tell her that I was okay. I heard her struggling against the monsters. I just wanted to tell her to play dead, just play dead. My mind raced to try to find a way to save my sister. How was I going to keep her alive? How was I going to save the last person on earth that actually cares about me?

The only way to save my sister was to catch the monsters by surprise. I had to be quick. Pushing myself off of the ground, I caught sight of my sister, now covered in blood, and I stumbled towards her. It was more difficult than I originally though it would be. My body was bleeding from top to bottom because of the nails of those creatures. It was painful to move an inch, let alone the twenty feet to the mob that held Zandriah. Nonetheless, I hobbled as quickly as I could, and was genuinely surprized when she broke free, and collapsed at my feet. The monsters were shocked at first, and didn't move, but we had to move fast if we were going to get out of here alive.

I slipped my sister's arm around my neck, but she pushed it away, smiling. She slipped something in my hand and whispered in my ear, "Go, I'll hold them off for as long as I can. Turn around, and run as fast as you can to the edge of the town, I'll be fine. I'm so sorry for dragging you into this town. Now you need to go without me, because I'm too weak. I'm just too weak now, sis."

Tears brimmed her knowing eyes as she pushed me away. We both knew what was going to happen. I didn't want to do it, but I swallowed my feelings, turned, and fled from the town. Hands were already grabbing out for my sister and I once again. I narrowly escaped, and painfully stumbled towards the edge of the town.

I ran as fast I could, my sides burning and my legs hurting from the unusually rigorous exercise that they have been getting lately. I tried to push the pain out of my mind, but for the first time, it wouldn't go away. I gritted my teeth as the edge of town started to get blurry. I had to get there. Zandriah would be disappointed if I didn't get there. I had a sudden burst of energy as I felt a claw brush my back. They had caught up to me. I needed to get to the edge of town… Why was it so far away? I could see the mountains getting bigger. I was thinking that if I could get to the mountains, I might be able to get away, or hide. Then, *THUD!* I took a chance and turned. I stopped and had to laugh breathlessly at one of the creatures on his butt, looking around, with a stupid look on his face. He scratched his head with one hand, rubbing his butt with the other as he stood. More creatures came and started to pound on an invisible barrier. I stumbled back, and toppled over.

"Avalon!" My sister screamed one last time. My spirits fell with my tears.

"Zandriah! Zandriah! Come on! We can go! *Zandriah!*" I cried out as loud as I could, but I knew it was too late. The creatures were carrying her off, and all I could do was watch them. I looked dejectedly down into my hand for the first time to see what she put in it. It was her necklace. Covered in blood and dirt, it still had a certain shine. I looked back, and saw that she had given up all hope. She looked into my eyes and yelled something lost in the air between us. Her body was shaking so badly with fearful sobs. I could see it from where I stood. Something wet touch my neck, and as I turned, my vision grew blurry, and the dim outline of a white tiger faded into blackness.

When I finally came to, there were rays of sunlight dancing on my face. I opened up my eyes, and saw damp rocks. *I'm in a cave.*

I slowly sat up, my body burned in protest. My wounds looked clean, but the weren't dressed. A shiver went through me as I realized that it was the white tigers who found me, and it was probably miles to the closest civilization. *Live civilization...*

"Go away, leave me alone. It's your fault my sister's in there, you should have been here to stop us. I hate you," I growled at them. I knew it was them. They were the voices that told us how to get down the mountain. Hell, if zombies are real why not this?

Are you sure it was our fault? You could've done what your mother told you to do, and gone around the damned town. It is your own fault, The tiger opened her mouth wide, and yawned, *but if you wish me to leave you, I will.*

"Unless you are going to join me, then just leave!" I cried.

I'll join you, She said lazily, as if we were talking about a morning stroll, or a breakfast outing. I watched her stretch out. Her muscles quivered and her demeanor changed from lazy to alert.

"I'm going to take a few minutes to recollect myself, find something to bandage my--"

No. We must leave now whether you want to or not. Dangers are lurking about.

"Fine, have it your way! I just lost my sister, not to mention my mother was just murdered, but hey! It's fine! Nobody gives a damn about my feelings! Not to mention the fact that I have several open wounds that could get infected," I spat.

Foolish! Zandriah is not lost forever. She did what she did to save you, and now you must find a way to save her in return. We do care about your feelings, we just don't have time to sit here and wallow in the path that your sister decided to take. The voice insisted. *Nor do we have time to dress your wounds, that'll have to wait.*

Facing away from her, towards the mouth of the cave was the town, and on the outskirts of it, the other white tiger. She was laying down, with her head poised. *I could almost trick my mind into thinking she was a statue.* I walked out of the cave, and sat down.

I am not a female, a deep, rumbling voice rolled into my thoughts.

"Sorry," I mumbled. *This whole mind reading thing is kind of creepy. Who else knows what I'm thinking?* I thought to myself.

Everyone. You suck at keeping your thoughts to yourself. You are possibly the easiest mind to get into. He grumbled. Even though his words were insulting, his voice was quite soothing.

"Okay. Well, this was fun, ut I gotta go. I have a sister to save." I slowly stood up and started walking. The female white tiger walked with me, while the male stayed behind.

Stick close to me, I don't want you getting too close to the town.

Chapter 4

I wasn't sad. I wasn't even mad. No, I was depressed. I was pissed off. I admit that the beast beside me was good company, but she wasn't Zandriah. She wasn't my sister. She was a stranger who tagged along on a journey that is sure to end in disaster.

As we skirted the town, ugly, snarling creatures flung themselves at the invisible barrier. They would look at me with anger and- could it be? -jealousy. I snarled back at them, even though the fear of them breaking the barrier and kid napping me was strong inside my belly. It startled me when I realized that they would *kid* nap me, just like they *kid* napped my sister. We were just kids. I tried to get further away from them, but I couldn't. The mountains surrounding the town pushed me near the barrier. I could see the mountains stop, and something brown start a couple miles ahead.

It was a huge forest, just like mom said. I stood there with my mouth open. When she said huge, I though that she meant it was a long way to the other side, but the trees were the biggest that I have ever seen. From here, I could see that they were at *least* twelve miles high, I could barely see the tops of the trees... and I was at least a mile and a half away. The stumps looked to be about two miles wide. I knew that this wasn't going to be an easy journey.

We have to move faster, we will never make it in time if we keep this pace! The white tiger said. I shook my head in frustration, but started to jog. In an effort to keep my mind off of the pain, I thought about everything that has happened since the night my house was burned down. I thought about mom. About Zandriah. I even thought about how perfect my life was before everything I knew as reality was ripped from me. Things I didn't know existed tore my life apart, and the firm ground I once stood upon crumbled to dust, leaving me to drown in the sorrows below.

So, after we get to the other side, will there be a town, or will there just be more mountains? More heartache? I wondered in my head.

"So-"

You'll find out soon enough. She answered. I could feel irritation rise into my chest. I tried to calm down, but there was just too much going on in my head. I walked the rest of that day, my body too worn out to jog. In all honesty, I felt too worn out to even walk. My head felt light from loss of blood, but when I tried to stop for the night, I was jabbed in the side.

We have to keep moving. There is a cave a little further up. We can both get a couple of hours of sleep there. I have a friend that is going to meet us there, and he'll give you the necessary tools to continue your journey. The white tiger insisted.

I struggled to my feet, and started walking again. After about ten minutes, I started to wonder how much longer we had to walk.

Here it--Run! The white tiger screamed in my head as she pushed me with her enormous paw. I stumbled, then started to sprint, not knowing what was happening.

"There they are! Come on, men; *let's get 'em!*" The very familiar voice boomed from behind.

Where are you! I screamed in my head to the white tiger. Not that it would help. My vision was beeing blurred by tears. My whole body was roaring with pain, and I knew that I wasn't going to be able to stay concious much longer. It was all too much.

Just run! She answered back. I tried to go faster.

"ARRRRG!" I didn't dare to look back and see what had gotten him. I already knew. I also knew that the people after me were out for blood. Any blood at this point.

One final roar pierced my heart as the knowledge of her passing on my behalf fell on my shoulders. I saw another cave that I might be able to hide in, but I kept running, fearing capture. It took me awhile to realize that I had another partner, running alongside me.

Hello, a deep voice rumbled, *my name is Lightning bird.* I took a moment to look over at Lightning bird. He was a hunter. A hunter is a breed of horse that is a cross between a Thoroughbred, a Cleveland Bay, and an Irish Draft. He had a short neck, and a compact body. He was all white, and had a big mark on his chest that looked like a bird, which is probably where he got his name.

Jump on my back; we'll be a lot quicker. He demanded, communicating in my head like the white tiger did. Normally, I would find that an easy request, but I wasn't sure I'd be able to in my current condition.

I have to try, I thought. He stopped just long enough for me to bend low, and catapult onto him, landing with my chest on his back. I grasped his hair, trying use it to pull myself up, but he jerked his head up, causing me to fall back onto the ground. As I sat there, he looked down at me with offense in his eyes. It didn't take a genius to know that he didn't like me tugging his hair out. I got up off the ground, embarrassed and tried again. This time, I found a small boulder, and we rushed over to it.

"Hurry men!" A voice said, causing me to panic. I jumped onto Lightning bird's back, and he galloped away. It felt like we were flying, he was like no other horse I have ever ridden. I realized very quick that riding bareback was very different than riding with a saddle. It was at that moment that I realized that he was white, when he should be a muddy brown. I thought back to all the other animals, and noticed one consistency.

Why is it that every animal that I've seen on this journey been white? I asked, *even the ones that I don't talk to are white.*

We are all looking out for you. We are here to make sure that no other animal can endanger you. While we are on the topic of protection, There is a sword and shield hooked onto my belt. Lightning bird said.

I looked down and, sure enough, there was a belt like strap where the cinch strap usually is. There was a shield on his left shoulder, and a sheathed sword on his right.

So, why do I need them? I've never used either! I said, hoping that he would say, 'Oh, those aren't for you!'

What do you mean? Your mom should've shown you! He snapped, irritated, *Never mind, we'll just have to teach you on the run. Grab the shield with one hand, and the sword with the other. Now.*

O-Okay. I said tentively. I didn't want to drop the weapons while trying to figure out how to properly grasp them. I looked back quickly, the people were just little dots on the horizon now. Lighting Bird jumped, and I nearly lost my balance. I clung onto the belt, riding all but sideways. Lightning Bird snorted, and was forced to run awkwardly until I was able to right myself. Back on his back, I redirected my attention to the task at hand.

I fumbled with the strap on the shield as I bounced on the horses back. If the situation wasn't so dire, I would laugh until I cried, but there was no time for that now, I needed to take a crash course on fighting for my life. I was starting to realize why nobody rides bareback anymore. My irritation was rising when the shield dropped like a rock out of my hands.

"NO! I dropped it; you'll have to go back!" I groaned, irritation turning into resentment. Why didn't my mom show my sister and I how to fight?

There's no time. Just grab the sword. I followed Lightning birds directions. The sword had a strap on it, and I struggled my left arm and head through the hole. It bounced uncomfortably on my back, but when I held it still, it rubbed my cuts.

You're bleeding on me Lightning bird's voice was a mixture of concern and irritation.

Yeah, well, that happens when you're covered in cuts.

The edge of the forest started getting rapidly closer. Anticipation clawed my insides when I saw a split between the trees. They were knitted so closely, though, that I would have to do some climbing. I decided if it would save my life, I'd be okay with it. Who knows, maybe Lightning Bird will jump over them. As we approached the tree roots, I saw that they were more like bumpy hills.

We're here. Lightning bird stopped, and craned his neck to see the tops of the root-hills. *You are on your own now. I need you to dismount. In the forest, you'll be completely on your own. No guide, nobody to save the day. You have to be strong.*

I looked at him in astonishment, I hadn't realized that he expected me to do this on my own. I just couldn't understand why all these people and creatures wanted so much from me. I had just lost everything, and now I was expected to make what I assumed to be a very hard and trying journey through a forest with trees that you couldn't see the tops of. Panic and anger set in as I threw the sword on the ground. Lightning Bird whinnied, and picked up his front feet, causing me to lose my balance. I fell hard on the ground, but he didn't see if I was okay. I scowled at him as he trotted away. At this point I wasn't too sure if he was a horse, or an ass.

Don't stray from the path, it'll cause you nothing but trouble. Lightning Bird's voice was as small in my head as his figure was to my eyes, which was now just a dot on the horizon. If my ears and mind hadn't been straining to hear some sort of sign, I would've never caught his message.

The climb up the roots only took a couple minutes, but it took all of my energy. I sat on top of one of the roots, and looked back at the town that held my sister. I could see the men and woman start to appear, first as blurry dots. They quickly became bigger as they ran at what seemed like full speed towards me. I rolled over, and pressed my stomache to the far side of the root, hoping that they couldn't see me. Before long, I could hear shouts and angry babbling. They didn't know where I was. Their voices faded, but I didn't dare to move until everything was silent once again. I carefully climbed down the root, trying not to obtain a sliver or twenty.

My feet finally hit the bottom, a sigh of relief escaped my lips. The gravel path was a little to the left of me, and I had a strange feeling that Lightning Bird knew exactly where it was, which meant one of two things. He has sent more than one person through here, or he's been through here before. Either way, the whole forest was nice and bright, the light filtered through the loosely placed trees everywhere.

I started walking, letting the gravel path guide me. I walked cautiously, not knowing what might jump out at or on me. I knew that I had to hunt for my food, whether I wanted to or not, I also knew that it was going to be considerably harder than hunting the white rabbits that were on the previous path.

As I got further into the forest, I noticed that the light around me did not dim, even though the trees grew dense, and blocked out the sun. I looked around to see where the light was coming from, and saw that the moss on the trees was glowing. I reached out and grabbed some, putting it in my pocket, just in case I needed light later.

Leave. Leave. LEAVE! HE! HE! HE! A high pitched voice screamed in my head. I couldn't tell if it was a boy, or a girl, but it had me worried. I unsheathed my sword, ready for anything.

"I won't leave, not until I get to the other side, and there is nothing you can do about it." I spat.

Fool! Leave now, or DIE! The voice chuckled insanely. I started to walk again, following the path that hopefully led to the other side of the forest. Looking around, I saw that the trees were getting smaller, looking up, they looked shorter. They looked almost normal.

TURN BACK NOW! FOOL! YOU WILL DIE IF YOU CONTINUE! TURN BACK! The voice screeched in my head, making me flinch. The more it spoke, the more frantic it seemed, almost as if it was desperate to get me out of there. I kept walking, pretending not to hear the voice.

My muscles tensed when I saw something move in between the trees. My fingers hurt from gripping the sword, and my head pounded as my heartbeat sped up. I swallowed as a black bear covered in scars lumbered out of the trees, and towered over me. It opened its great jaws, and let out a roar that sent shivers of fear through me. I took a deep breath, and straightened up.

"Move," I demanded, "Or I'll kill you." The bear called my bluff by charging at me. I threw up my arms, temporarily forgetting that I had a sword at my disposal. I could feel the impact of the bear, and fell to the ground, my bones rattling in my skin. I was able to pull myself to my hands and knees. Looking up, I saw blood gushing out of his side, where my sword had nicked him. He looked straight into my eyes, and I saw rage mixed with pain, but I mostly saw grief. I knew that this was no bear, but something more.

He charged again. This time I jumped out of the way. I spun quickly, and then slashed awkwardly at his back. He reared up, and then turned on me. I lunged forward as fast as I could, and buried the sword where his heart should be. Whether or not he even had a heart was beyond my knowledge. He roared loudly in agony. His final attempt to stop me was to swipe out his paw, which caught me off guard, and I went sprawling to the ground, screaming.

I heard a great **thud!** And saw the black bear on his back. Walking up to him, cautiously, painfully, i pulled my blood-drenched sword out of his chest. I walked over to the edge of the path, and wiped my sword as clean as possible on a patch of grass.

I started to walk away again when the voice whispered, *this is not the end, I will get you. You will not pass. Nobody does, unless I say they can, and I say that you can't.*

"Lovely." I said, annoyed that this thing thought that he could stop me.

My next obstacle came later that day, when I came to a fork in the path. I sat for a while, deciding which path to take. The mysterious voice had become a very welcome visitor. He was funny to listen to. Crazy, but funny. Not to mention he kept throwing out challenges, making me stop to think. Like the one right now. I was eating a brown rabbit that I had caught (Not everything was white now, letting me know that I was on my own) when I noticed that he had diverged the paths. It was actually a very hard challenge, because they can either both go to the town, or neither could head there.

After I finished my meal, I started to walk. Not to either of the paths, but right in the middle. I walked to where I could see both paths, but if anyone or thing was to wander down it, I'd be able to hide easily.

"Darek! See either of those brats?" A female voice carried over the path, and washed over me. I looked back and saw that Darek was a few feet behind me, and I crouched down lower, slowly moving away from him. I knew that if I could, I should try to avoid a fight.

"Nothing!" He yelled back. I took another step. CRACK! I accidentally stepped on a twig when I was looking behind me.

I jumped on the opposite path and ran as fast as I could away from the shouts and demands. I knew that if I didn't go faster, or find a place to hide, they would catch up. I tried to go faster, but I was already sprinting. I thought about ditching the sword and shield, but that would be stupid. I would have no protection if they still caught up. I couldn't stop and dive in the bushes because they would see me.

"I'm right on her tail!" A different voice said. It was definitely male, and he sounded big. Real big. I made a split second decision.

I turned and rammed into the guy without looking. It shouldn't have been a shock that he was just as big as he sounded, but I couldn't move because of the fear for a second. I threw my shield on the ground, and did what I thought could pass for a roundhouse kick, and watched as he fell to the ground, unconscious. I winced as my ankle throbbed. Another man brought down a sword of his own. I rolled clumsily out of the way, and stuck my sword into his chest. He gurgled a bit, and fell to the ground.

I felt a sharp pain in my back as somebody kicked me. I turned on her. She kicked my arm, and sent my sword flying. I rolled again as the woman tried to land a punch. I saw out of the corner of my eye that my shield was ruined, and the dead man's sword was only feet from me. I propelled myself off of my belly with my feet, and ran to pick it up. I flung it over my head like a hammer, and let it go at just the right time. It hit her in her chest, a little to the left. I spun around in a full three sixty to see if there was anybody else was around. The rest, it seemed, had run away.

After being unable to find my own sword, I stomped back over to the dead woman and took the sword out of her chest. Stepped to the side of the path, where grass grew timidly on the edges, and cleaned it off as good as possible. The mysterious voice from before spoke yet again in my head.

Take good care of that sword; it once belonged to a fearless leader. The paths came together, the bodies vanished, and my shield lay by the path, destroyed. I went to put the new sword in my old sheath, and found that my original sword had somehow found its way back into its sheath. I looked around and found a second sheath next to my ruined shield. Odd, where did that come from? And what had happened to everything else?

Sighing, I looked at the new sword curiously, and then started to walk down the path, wondering what fearless leader the voice was talking about.

Chapter 5

I didn't want another run in with anybody for a while, so I decided to jog lightly for the rest of the dwindling day, and to walk through the night.

As the sun rose slowly through the trees, I trudged through my exhaustion, trying to get closer to the end of the nightmarish journey as fast as humanly possible. Hours and hours later, when night fell yet again, I abandoned all thought of making camp, and fell fast asleep on the side of the path.

Before I knew it, morning came, with the usual aching bones and body. I got up slowly. After making sure everything was as it should be, I left, leaving no hint that I was even there.

I walked for hours with no food, water, or foe, in sight. My stomach started to growl and churn in pained hunger. I looked hopelessly around for food or water or any way out. I looked straight ahead to see how far the next bend in the road was, and was delighted to see a small light straight ahead. I didn't run, because oddly I had no urge to. I didn't know if it was a trick from the mysterious voice, who I haven't heard from since the fight, or if it was real.

After about half an hour of following the path, I was glad that I didn't choose to run, even though by now I knew that it was no mirage. However, I was anxious to get out as fast as possible, so I changed my pace to a slight jog.

Suddenly I stopped in my tracks, remembering a key detail in this bizarre journey. I pulled out the three necklaces, wondering why they were such a big deal. True, they had always been a part of my family's life, but they were just pretty little trinkets given to my sister and me by our mother. Then, of course, there was the one she kept for herself. In all honesty, I had forgotten about them. They didn't have any real value to me.

Yet. No value to you yet. The female voice sounded more like bells than any voice I had ever heard. But who did it belong to? And why did she say that it wasn't important *yet?* Oh well. Whoever it is, it wasn't important.

I slipped the necklaces into my pocket, All but one… The one my mom always wore around her neck. I felt tears start to burn back of my eyes. My mind went back to better times. To happier times. I miss her so much. Why couldn't I have stayed? Why did she make me go?

I started to walk again, but as I walked I had the urge to turn around, to just turn around and go back to my sister, rescue her, and go home. But I didn't. I knew that I needed to continue, to keep going until I reached my destiny, and say the words that my mom told me to say. What was it? Rise again? No, there was more to it. Rise once again? No, there was still something missing. It was something like 'rise, live again'.

"Rise, live again." I whispered to myself. Sounded right enough to me.

I walked as fast as I could away from the memory, then I started to jog, then sprint. I just wanted to get away from the horrible feeling. Just as I felt that I was about to out run it, I stopped. I didn't know where the feeling was coming from, but I would fight it, and I would win.

As the feeling gnawed at me, I looked up ahead and saw the end of the forest was very near. I decided to walk the rest of the way to the edge of the forest. The voice came back as I reached the end.

Last chance. You could turn around, and never come back. You could be out of here in less than a day; all you have to do is turn back, and promise to never return. I knew I shouldn't, and even though every fiber in my body wanted to turn around and go back, I didn't turn around, not even one last time, to look at the path. I knew that if I did, I would turn back, and then I would never get out of here.

"I promise," I said, smiling ahead, "That I would never do a thing like that," I stepped out of the forest, and away from the furious roars. As soon as I stepped out, the voice silenced.

"What in the..." my voice trailed as my eyes adjusted to the burning light. There wasn't anything there, no buildings, no trees, not even a blade of grass. Just miles and miles of open desert. I took a deep breath and muttered, feeling rather stupid, "Rise, live again." nothing happened.

I cleared my throat, and spoke as clearly as I could, "Rise, live again."

My patience snapped, and I yelled in frustration, "Oh for goodness sake when I say 'rise, live again' why can't you just rise and live once again!" as if I angered them, I felt a grumbling under my feet. I unsheathed my swords, ready for a fight, barely able to stand up as the earth quaked. Even as I did so, I heard the rumbling of laughter and reunion.

Then I saw the most horrid, yet most beautiful, sight in my life. My eyes widened, and my breath was taken from out of my chest. I wanted to scream, or to move, but found myself unable to do so.

Chapter 6

I stood as still as possible. These things weren't human, nor any creature I've ever seen. Even in the fiction books that I have read. They were like a cross of a human-skeleton from the waist up, with huge skeleton paws, much like a werewolf. They had a horse or mule hide,but instead of hooves they had talons. And they were as tall as normal trees, some smaller, some even taller! I tried so hard not to show any fear, but I felt so small. Nothing was adding up. The journey, these ugly, yet kind of beautiful, creatures, and the sword that once belonged to a great ruler, or whatever.

One of the things knelt down on his front knees, and I slashed out my sword. He dodged it easily, and chuckled. He *chuckled*. Although it shook the earth, and rumbled deep like a purr or a growl, it was somehow distinctly a merry little chuckle.

"Wow, hunny, careful where you're swinging that thing, you could hurt somebody, or yourself. If you hurt yourself, then what good would you be?" his jaw moved weirdly, and I was still trying to figure out how it stayed on without ligaments or muscles, or better yet, how he was able to speak without any vocal chords, as the other things chuckled with him.

"Who are you?" I asked slowly, careful not to stammer. As soon as I asked, the things burst out laughing, nearly shattering my ear drums. Still holding my swords, I pressed my hands against my ears.

"We have no name." He bellowed simply, then his voice got sad, and empty. "We are usually called the ugly things. Every body's afraid of us."

I felt sympathy creeping into my heart. I didn't want to hear this. "But, you guys are so beautiful. I don't see how anybody can say that you are ugly!" It didn't slip, I meant every word, and I was furious that anybody would dare to call these creatures outright ugly! "What is your name?" I asked.

"We don't have any of those either." Although unable to show emotion on its bone face, the creature looked like he was about to cry. The dark shadows in his all seeing empty eye sockets went to a darker shade of black, and his breath hitched for a second before he summoned himself up, and towered high, and proud, like he should.

"Well, I am going to call you guys the desert beauties." I said, knowing that I couldn't live with calling them creatures. "We'll figure out actual names for you and your species later, but right now, I want to know why I am here. Please." I added at the end.

"You should know, Alana!" The creature laughed. Everything seemed to click. "Although, I must say, you've changed since the last time we've seen you."

"I am not Alana, Alana was my mother. My name is Avalon." I whispered slowly.

"Speak up, hunny, we can't hear you," one of the Desert beauties growled kindly, her voice like Bricks.

"My name," I started, a little louder, but just as slowly, "Is Avalon and Alana was my mother."

The shock on one's face was almost more than I could bear. It's jaw hung open, and its head tilted slightly back, "Then where is your sister?" A different one said, a boy with a booming voice. "Avalon," He said when I didn't answer, "Where is Zandriah?"

I stared at him, silently begging him not to make me answer as tears threatened to make an appearance.

"She's not in the death town is she? Nobody has gotten out of there, not even the people who built the town, and starved to death there. They rose up as hideous creatures, and think only of three special necklaces. The ones that can kill anything, or give rebirth to any creature, if you say the right words," The desert beauty with a voice like bricks rambled on, and was making little sense.

I pulled the necklaces out of my pocket, "you mean these ones?" I asked, "And this one? I asked, lifting the necklace out of my shirt, so that they could see them.

"Tell us now how you got those!" A girl demanded. "Those are supposed to be in the hands of your mother, you little thief!"

The sight of the necklaces sent all of the desert beauties into an uproar. They were saying how I am a thief, how they felt there was something wrong since they first saw me. They were stomping and throwing their hands around. Their movements were fast, not slow like you would think they would be.

The one that I met first quieted them, and then he bent back down on his knees and asked, "How did you get those? Why doesn't Alana have them?"

"I have them because my mom was killed, and my sister is trapped in a town that she can't get out of." I choked, just loud enough for them to hear me.

A deadly silence came over everybody. No one knew what to say. I didn't want to say anything to anybody, because I felt extremely offended that they would just assume that I stole these necklaces, and that I am a thief.

"I am so sorry." The girl that had a voice like bricks said. "Please forgive me!"

"Just tell me how you know that I have a sister, and how I can get her back. If I can get her back." I corrected myself.

"We know your sister because your mother told us about her. She would visit us every summer, until you guys were born. She came down to us one last time, when she was pregnant with Zandriah; she said that one day, you two would defeat the ultimate power. Of course, that ultimate power is actually a very powerful human. His name is Bane. He towers above everybody, and ordered you, your sister, and your mother killed." One of the desert beauties said, sadly.

"Well." was all that I could seem to say.

"After your sister was born," He continued, "your mother had your necklace separated into two necklaces, now they must be combined to their fullest power, again."

"How am I supposed to get them combined, and save my sister?!" I screamed. My temper, and confusion, was rising.

"Come with us, we'll help you forge the two single necklaces, then we can come up with a plan to kill the creatures in the town, and save your…save your…" The girl who was talking trailed off as she looked at one of my swords. She was looking at the sword that belonged to the 'fearless leader'. "Where did you get that sword?" Her voice had held a little hint of worry and excitement.

"I had a little bit of trouble with some people back in the woods." I told them my story from back in the woods.

"The voice you talk about is called The Confuser. He tries to make people turn back, and usually they do, then he traps them in the forest, where they slowly go crazy, and he stays sane in return." A boy said.

"That is so cruel!" I whispered.

"That is just how it is, now we need to get those necklaces forged, and save your sister." a girl said when she saw that the boy was going to go on.

The desert beauty who talked to me first waved his arms in one long, sweeping gesture. With a rumble and a great earth quake that knocked me on my butt, a whole village made out of compacted sand rose from the depths of the earth, and stood strong, as if it had been there for ages, and would be there for ages to come.

"Follow me," He said. It was about now that I decided he was the leader of the whole group, so his nickname would be 'Boss'. I did as Boss bid me to do, and followed him into one of the giant houses. The door of the house was so large, that I couldn't have reached it on a twelve foot ladder. As it was, the desert beauties were so large that I had to run to keep up with them.

"Here," Boss said, and extended a skeleton werewolf paw. I climbed into it gingerly, not at all comforted by his long, sharp claws. The tips alone were as big as I was. Nevertheless, I made it safely onto the huge table unscathed. I noticed that everything around me was my size. There were even smaller tables that were my size. Heck, there was a whole blacksmith setup on here in my size too. Not to mention the maps.

I turned to ask them why everything seemed to be in human size, when I noticed something peculiar. They all looked a little smaller. Then I realized that they were a little smaller, a lot smaller actually. Before my very eyes these creatures were silently miniaturizing. I muffled a gasp as they stepped onto the table one by one, and maintained the size of your average horse.

"We can shrink for small amounts of time, but it is painful and takes a lot out of us, so we must hurry," Boss said to me. I nodded, too amazed to say anything. "The necklaces if you will."

I handed the necklaces over, and watched as he walked calmly over to an anvil. He set the necklaces down, one on top of the other, and stepped back. The desert beauty with a voice like bricks went up to the anvil. I decided to nickname her 'Brick', and hoped she wouldn't find it offensive if she ever found out.

Curiosity got to me, and I walked up beside Brick. Her eyes were closed and she was mumbling something as she waved her paw like hands over the necklaces. They didn't glow or anything, they just seemed to melt together. Smiling, she stopped chanting and lifted them up.

"There you go," Brick said, handing me the necklace. I slipped it over my head for safe keeping.

"Now, we need to figure out a plan," Boss said from behind us, "Come, and we'll go over a few, and figure out which one we like best."

Twenty minutes later we were going over the finishing touches for saving my sister.

"I think that if I go through the back, then I might have a chance. I might be able to get in there, silently kill anything that gets in my way, find Zandriah, and get out," I said, sounding a lot more confident than I felt.

"Then that is what we'll go with, it's the easiest to do, even if it sounds like a lot. Don't forget to give Zandriah her necklace, and keep it on you until you get it to her." Boss reminded me for the hundredth time.

"Yes, Boss," I said impatiently, "I know."

Chapter 7

A mouse would be jealous of how quietly I snuck into the town. Not even the weeds I walked on knew that I was there. That was the plan. To get in as quietly as possible. I slowly crept through the shadows of the houses.

"You there! What do you think you are doing?" I froze. "Yeah, you, in the shadows, get out of there, or I will go in there and cut you to pieces!" A rough voice grated over my ears, making me fight violent chills that speared into my body.

I started to slowly go for my sword, when a creature burst from the shadows right in front of me. "Please, don't! I am just doing as I was told," it was a voice that I recognized all too much.

"Zandriah," I whispered under my breath.

"I knew we shouldn't have let you live! You little…" I unsheathed my sword and threw it over my head like an axe. The creature gurgled as it fell to the ground. I ran to the creature and pulled the sword out of its chest.

"Come on Zandriah, we got to get out of here!" I urged, and lunged for her hand.

All she did was stare at me and whisper, "You came back!"

"I did, yes, now come on!" I was on the edge of panicking. I didn't want to be found.

"No, it's impossible to leave here without some charm, or talisman, or something. We are stuck here now." She whispered, her voice was so hollow.

"I know that, now come on! I have what we need, here put this on!" I draped the newly forged necklace over her head, and then tugged on her arm.

She looked down at it curiously, and followed me at a run towards the edge of the town. The monsters that captured my sister were running after us. We picked up our pace to a sprint. I knew that they were hot on our heels by the sounds of their feet ker-thunking against the hard ground.

I looked back to see how close they were, and tripped. As I hit the ground I heard a crack, and felt it in my arm. I felt my leg bruise and welt on the side of the calf, and a long cut from sliding on a sharp rock stretched from my hip to my armpit. Adrenaline kicked in and I stood up against the pain and started to sprint again. My sister was already a couple of strides ahead of me. I saw her reach the edge of the forest and just as I was about to reach it, a hand grabbed my torn shirt.

I struggled against the grip as more reached for me. Zandriah held out her hand and I felt friendly fingers seize my arm like a lifeboat in the ocean. Together we pulled and tugged and finally I was on the other side of the barrier. I smiled at Zandriah but knew something was wrong. I looked around and sure enough there was one of those things on our side of the barrier looking at me with surprise. I reacted quickly and slit its throat. It fell to the ground and turned into dust. The rest of the things thudded against the almighty invisible barrier.

"That was easier than I thought it would be!" I said gleefully, and turned to Zandriah. Her head was bowed, and I realized that I haven't seen her face yet. I didn't check to see if she had purple tinted eyes, or if her eyes were normal, like I was told to do. I had my sword ready, hoping that I wouldn't have to slice and dice her too.

She looked up, and to my relief, her eyes were normal. I sheathed my sword, and my relief faded. In the excitement of getting out of the town and then killing the uninvited guest on our side of the barrier, I hadn't really paid attention to her condition, and I noticed that even though her eyes are just fine, the rest of her face was a way different story. She had a deep scratch on her left cheek, and the rest of her face sported bruises everywhere.

I looked down at her bare arms. They were deep red and told a story of immense pain and suffering. I cringed. They were small cuts, but there were so many, and they were all intertwined and braided together.

"They tortured me into giving them information. I didn't know what they were talking about most of the time, and that angered them." Zandriah answered the unasked question with a quavering voice. She wasn't able to look me in the eyes, and she kept trying to hide the cuts and bruises with her hands. "They kept saying how someone named Bane would come and rescue them, but some don't think so. They said that they were told to build a town. After they built it, all their horses and cattle, and food, and water were poisoned.

"They said that they starved there because of Bane. Who is Bane?" Zandriah had stopped to take a breath and wipe away her tears. I didn't know where to start.

"Bane," I said, gently guided her towards the woods, "Is an evil guy that has taken over a lot of land. He is not a good person, and he needs to be stopped."

As soon as we took a couple of steps into the woods Zandriah looked at me and said, "Somebody doesn't want us in here, we should go around."

"No, let's not," I said firmly and then told her why, and what happened to me when I first came through here, "I think he gets weaker when somebody gets to where he or she needs to go. He isn't as loud as he was before. Come on, we need to get to the other side." I said, hoping that she and I had the strength to get through the forest.

"Okay, but I am still not sure." Zandriah walked a little slow, and I let her.

"Something doesn't seem right; I haven't heard the voice in a long time." I said, after a few hours of walking.

"Oh, I hear it," Zandriah whispered. She looked to the end, and her eyes widened.

"Don't run, it's further than it looks. Just keep the pace slow and steady, don't get ahead of yourself, we still have a couple days left and we are both injured." I kept walking at a slow, but steady, pace.

"There is no way! I can see the light right there, it is so close!" I let her go at a limping jog, just to show her that she is wrong. I stayed painfully at her heels, cradling my broken arm, until she stopped at sundown.

"Now that you've stopped, why don't we make camp, I'm a bit tired, and I hurt." I laid down on the path as carefully as possible, and she flopped right next to me. My arm throbbed and pulsed and was about twice the size as normal.

"Aren't we going to actually make camp? You know, with blankets and a fire…and food?" she asked hopefully.

"No. Here," I said tossing her a slice of bread out of my oversized pants pocket. I watched as she devoured it. I turned over and fell into an exhausted sleep.

Chapter 8

Silent violence. Terrible sights. Unbearable pain. Choking. Wheezing.... Laughing. Oh the laughter. The terrible, terrible, unbearable, laughter. In my ears, in my head, surrounding me with it's terrible feelings. Hungry, hungry for more. More pain, more terrible sights, oh that laughter was the bane of my existence. I hated it. It needed to stop. I clenched my teeth, and lunged forward with the blade in my hand.

"Avalon! Avalon! Wake up! We've got trouble!" My sister woke me from my sleep, and I was thankful.

"What?" I was still confused on what she meant by 'trouble', when I felt a sharp blow between my shoulders. I yelped as my injured arm throbbed in rapid pain.

I was wide awake now, and saw that a big black bear towered above us. It had a bald spot on its heart, and I knew, without anybody telling me that it was the bear from before. I grabbed my swords from my waist, and threw one in the air toward Zandriah. She caught it and looked nervously at the bear.

I lunged forward, only to be swiped by a powerful paw that sent me sprawling to the ground, making my bad arm bend unnaturally. I could see Zandriah from where I was, slashing at the bear with fear. The bear swiped her aside too, as if she weighed nothing. It started towards her again. I got up, and jumped on the back of the bear, hoping to distract it. It worked. The bear reared back, outraged. I sliced it at the neck, and it went down. I raised my sword, and plunged it into the beasts back.

I sheathed my sword, and grabbed my sister by the arm saying, "Come on, we got to go, before it wakes back up!"

"It won't wake back up, trust me, you killed it." Zandriah said, skeptical.

"That's what I said the first time I thought I killed it. It fooled me once, but it won't fool me again. Like the old saying, fool me once, shame on you, fool me twice, shame on me. One difference, next time I might not live to be shamed." I said, trying to get her moving, all the while.

"Oh." Was all she seemed to be able to say, and she followed.

We set off at a pained jog, the dream from before still vividly playing in my head. Why had I dreamt of it? Where did it come from? Why was that person laughing?

I tried to put it out of my head. It was just a dream…. Right? Even if it was more than a dream, it didn't matter, there were more pressing matters at hand right now, like getting out of the forest. The next two days went by painfully. My arm was still bent at a bit of an angle, and I had sprung a fever.

"We should be nearing the end now, a little further, Zandriah, you're going to make it." I urged her, really just trying to convince myself that we would make it before our wounds killed us. I stumbled, leaning on Zandriah, barely able to stand

"Let's make camp, we can finish the journey tomorrow." I stuttered, realizing that I was too exhausted to go on.

"Fine, but if you keep having fits like you did the last couple of nights, I'm going to wake you up, and we are going to finish the journey then." Zandriah sounded extremely worried as she looked at my feverish state. I fell into a fit of dreams immediately.

I plunged the sword into the laughing man, and I knew why they called him Bane. Because he was such a nuisance. I watched him fall to the ground, gagging.

I bent down towards him and said, "That was for all those people that you sent to the death town. They starved to death, you know? They had a slow death, and they still think that you are the best leader in the world, or at least some do. And this," I continued, pulling the sword out, then plunging it back into his gut, creating more blood, "Is for my sister, who I promise you, I will find!"

"Noooo!" I jumped up to my feet, pulled out my swords, and looked around for my sister, like a mother for her lost baby. My head was pounding, and I couldn't see straight. Everything was blurry and fish-eyed.

"Zandriah!" I fell on the ground. My sister was gone, yet again.

"Avalon, you'll be okay!" I felt two arms come around me. I felt a lot better all of a sudden. Then they were gone. I looked up and saw that she wrote something in the air. It read;

It's time to carve your destiny, sister, let the land guide you to me, I love you.

My fever came back, and so did my pain, as the words faded away. I looked to where the rest of my journey was waiting. I fought to stand up, and walked out of the woods. I was depressed and saw her face as I walked the rest of the way. Sometimes I heard her voice, sometimes I saw her. Other times I felt her touch me. Each time I tried to talk to her, she turned into the creatures of that horrid little town.

I reached the end of the forest, and passed out. When I woke up, my arm was fixed, and my fever had gone down. The bruises on my leg had disappeared, and the scratch on my side was now just a faint scar. I fought back tears. I had just found my sister, and then I lost her again. I got out of the bed that I was laying on, and walked out of the little make-shift hut. There was a bunch of creatures here now.

I marched past the desert beauties, and all of the other animals that were demanding where Zandriah was. Only one animal could come. I walked up to Lightning bird. He had my swords with him.

I hopped on. *To the mountains in the North.* I said, somehow knowing that was where we needed to go. The necklace around my neck was banging against my skin. I felt something in my pocket, I didn't know what it was, and it wasn't there before, but I was too busy to care.

Chapter 9

We rode at night, and slept the day away. This helped us get ahead, using the moonless dark as a mask.

Anger and pain were now welcome visitors. I didn't care if I was silent. I was vigilant. I wasn't about to lose the friend who was willingly carrying me on his back, and I knew if I talked it would be words of hate and anger, and he would leave me. I was also not ready to lose the last person who shared my blood and really cared about me.

My sister was the one thing that kept me sane. I would've given up long ago if it wasn't for her. I won't give up now. I won't let the enemy have any satisfaction. If they kill my sister, then I will slowly kill each one. I will not show them mercy.

We were brought into a battle that tore my family apart. One that I didn't even know existed, until that fateful night. I won't lose another person I love. I refuse.

We made it to the foot of the mountain, and I dismounted Lightning Bird.

I wish you well; the rest of your journey must be made alone. Good-bye, my sweet Avalon, may your mother's spirit be with you as you travel. Lightning Bird turned, and I started my journey, the white horse fading behind me, back to where she belonged.

What is she doing? A voice inside my head said, fear around the edges.

I don't know, let's follow her, maybe she can lead us to food. Another said, they sounded like little kids. The first sounded like a girl, the other like a boy.

Allen? the first one said.

What, Irish? Allen asked, much like a concerned parent.

I want mama! Irish wailed in my head.

"You and I both, Irish." I said, hoping to lure whoever was speaking out of their hiding place.

You can hear me?! Irish, who by now I have figured out is a girl, said, sounding excited.

Yup. I said in my mind, still hoping that they would come out.

Two small white wolf cubs stumbled out, and Irish asked, *Can we come with you, please?*

Sure, I would love that, but I might get into some trouble, if you can handle a little fighting. I said, and laughed when one jumped on my shoelace. *My name is Avalon.*

I knew instantly that the one who jumped on my shoelace was Allen, trying to show off to his sister.

When I say two small cubs, I mean that they are about twice the size of a Labrador pup. Their teeth looked as sharp as knives, and their paws were way too big for their body. The smallest one, Irish, had Irish green eyes and Allen had Ice blue eyes, making his stare twice as intense.

We used to have a different mommy. She was as tall as you. She was a human too. Her name was Alana. We would visit her every day at the edge of the forest, and she would feed us. The last time we went there, though, it was burnt down, and it was a big pile of ash. Irish said, sounding very sad. I was surprised, but I felt obliged to tell them the truth for some reason.

She was my actual mommy. I lived in that house. I said back, and the two wolves cocked their heads to the left.

I started to go up the mountain, with Irish and Allen close at my heels. I was glad that they had come out of their hiding place, now I wouldn't feel as lonely.

Still, it would be hard to feed three mouths.

My mind was racing, trying to figure out how to feed all three mouths, and asking myself why my mom hadn't told me that she had been feeding two little wolves. Well, now I know where the scraps and leftovers have been going. Come to think of it, mom did make a lot of meat. she also bought too much to eat, and the extra would mysteriously vanish.

I kept climbing, making sure that it was at a pace that Irish and Allen could keep up with. We walked for about 5 hours.

* * * * *

I have never been so mentally exhausted in my life! We've been climbing the mountains for a couple weeks now, and Irish was funny, but she *never stopped talking!* Sometimes I hoped that I would go deaf…. Not that that would help, being as the voice was in my head, and not in my ears. While Irish was talking, I was wondering why Allen wasn't. And, to put the bow around the present, they both got bigger as every day passed, and as they got bigger, they got hungrier.

They were learning to hunt for their own food, and would let me share with them. Usually they would only catch a few rabbits, but they would occasionally catch a mountain goat. My main worry was that they would either turn back, get killed by *my* enemies, or would get killed by a mountain lion, or something.

Irish and Allen grew into their paws, and they were as big as the white tigers now. They would have to leave every few hours to catch something to eat. Even though they had grown extremely smart, Irish still talked like she did when she was a cub, And Allen still, well, he had just about grown up, mentally, by the time that I had met them.

Stop talking for a second, Irish, I hear something! Allen snapped at his little sister. Sure enough, there was a rustling in the bushes, and a dagger flew inches from my face as I drew out my swords.

"Come on, Men, GET HER!" A female voice said.

Irish, Allen, Go! Get back into the shadows and leave, now! They did as I told, creeping into the shadows. I waited for the men and women to jump out of the bushes. They did only seconds after the wolves had made their retreat to the shadows. I sliced out with one of my swords, and it nicked the woman that was closest to me. I looked quickly back behind her, and saw that there was no way I would be able to kill all of these people by myself.

I need help! I thought to myself, as I turned and stabbed a man that snuck his way behind me. I felt a searing pain on the back of my knee as I fell to the ground. Getting quickly to my feet, I turned, and sliced the neck of the woman I had nicked before. She screamed, and the remaining army went into a rage.

The closest man threw down his sword and fell down to the ground next to his dead companion. I knew at once that I had just killed their leader, but why had it been so easy?

I didn't have any time to dwell on the question. The man grabbed his sword, stood back up, and brought his sword down on me. I had barely enough time to put my sword up to block it. I kicked him in the stomach, making him fall back into the others. As he slid off the side of the mountain, he reached out his hands blindly, and dragged four more people to their deaths.

One of the men roared, and he charged at me, the others close behind him. They all surrounded me, pointing the tips of their swords at me.

"Don't move, or we will kill you," One woman raged.

"Why can't we just kill her now?" a voice whined.

"You know why!" Another said.

They started to argue, a couple of them lowering their swords. I took advantage of the moment. I swung the sword around my head, hitting their weapon, and disarming many of the men and women.

I sliced out at arm's length, killing two men, and then I ducked as four more jumped, swords outstretched, and they collided, killing each other.

Maybe I don't need help. These men are morons! They were probably given swords and told that they were knights. I thought, Even though there were still a lot of men left, more men filling in the spots of the dead.

One of the women demanded, "Where did you get that sword!"

I slashed out at her, and she expertly avoided me. I turned and slashed out at more men, killing two, but one was also able to maneuver out of my way.

At that point, many men and women turned and ran back down the mountain side, many tripping and falling the rest of the way, dead.

Now only four remained. Three men and one woman.

"The woman asked you a question, answer!" The man to my left barked at me.

"Why should I?" I asked, and went to do a downward slash at him. He narrowly avoided it, clearly surprised that I could get that close to hurting him.

I turned and did an upward slash, and ended up slashing a man's arm, then I brought down my other sword, effectively slashing his other arm, and disarmed him while he was busy clutching his injured arm.

I saw out of the corner of my eye that the man to my left was bringing his sword down, and I blocked his attack, then, still holding off his attack, I kicked out my left leg, making contact with the man I had slashed at the arms, and I sent him tumbling down the mountain. I slashed out my other sword at the man that I was still holding his sword with mine, and I slashed his stomach. I jabbed him again with the sword, and he fell to the ground, dead.

I felt an excruciating pain in my left shoulder, and then I heard an angered roar.

I turned in time to see Irish and Allen take down the remaining man. I saw that they had left the woman untouched.

They backed up into the shadows again, waiting to help me, if needed.

I looked straight into the woman's eye. I knew that she would be difficult to kill. And that there was only one sure way of killing her, although I didn't like it.

I started to feel pain in my right leg. I knew that I had to stay crouched, so that I wouldn't provoke her to make the first move.

Our eyes stayed locked, neither dared to blink an eye. The pain in my left leg was growing, but I didn't care, not now. We stayed still, not moving for about half an hour, and I had enough, I wanted to move, and I could tell she felt the same way.

I took stock of my surroundings, noting that the mountainside was to my back, and the mountain's edge was to hers. I summoned all my strength, as she made the first move towards me. She was fast, almost as fast as I was. I jumped straight up, and then did a back flip in mid air onto a boulder that sat steadily on the mountain. I watched as she collided painfully into the boulder, unable to stop herself in time, and then I jumped down off the rock. I raised my sword before she could turn around, and beheaded her in one semi-swift move.

I cringed away from her body, not wanting to see the blood. Then, still not looking at the body, I turned and walked away, Irish and Allen on my heels. I knew that they had watched, and I hadn't wanted them to. But they sat and watched, and now even Irish was silent.

Chapter 10

Two days of hell. Two days by myself. Allen and Irish took off the night after the battle. When I woke up the next morning to find them gone, I couldn't fight back the tears of loneliness. I wanted them back so bad. I never even thanked them for saving me.

It was a punch in the gut to find them gone. There was a part of me that knew they would leave after the first battle, but there was a part that was hoping that they would stay with me forever. I knew that if I was to survive until I got to my sister, I would have to go solo. I also knew that the wolves wouldn't come back, but if they did, then I would have to make sure they left, even if that meant hurting their feelings.

I looked at my waist to make sure that I still had my swords, wiped away a fresh tear, and kept going over the endless mountain range.

My left shoulder no longer hurt. It turned out that the man had kicked, not stabbed or cut me. It was right after the last battle that I realized that I was going to have to be more careful, and learn how to handle myself better. Unfortunately, there was nobody to train with.

I looked up at the next, and hopefully last, mountain I had to climb. I took a deep breath, and took the first step up. I knew that I had to climb all the mountains, cross whatever had to be crossed on the other side, and get my sister back before they killed her.

I had gone over many battle strategies in my head while I had been alone. The fact that I didn't know where my sister was being kept didn't discourage me. I just wanted my sister to be free. I didn't care if I died finding and freeing her, but she deserved to be free.

I was becoming faster at climbing the mountains, being able to climb one side in just over two days. And even though I only got a couple of hours of sleep, it didn't bother me. The less sleep, the fewer nightmares.

The nightmares had gotten worse. Whenever I went to sleep, I would see my sister being brutally beaten. The men hurting her asked her questions that she didn't know.

How long has your mother had those necklaces? Why did she give them to you? Why does your sister carry all of them? Where is your sister?

The questions were endless, and the beatings got worse whenever she said that she didn't know. At night she would be chained to a wall, and left there with no food or water. You could see her ribs through her tattered clothes.

I would go to her in my dreams. I would sing to her, and talk to her. I tried to bring her as much comfort as possible, until the guards came, then I would wake up. I desperately wished that they were just nightmares, and not actually real. I didn't want to be the cause of her pain. I should've watched her more closely!

As I climbed the mountains, I had questions nagging at me; *what do they mean when they ask where I was? I was with her! Could she have wondered into the forest while she was watching out? And what were they talking about, me caring both necklaces?*

I wanted to just shake it off, but I couldn't. It was the worst feeling in the world, knowing that I should be in the cell with her, and instead I'm climbing these stupid mountains. I hated it!

The journey got worse with every step I took. All the bones in my body felt bent and broken. I've come to such great emotional turmoil, that I had to stop thinking at times to stop myself from just jumping off the mountain.

After all was said and done, though, at the end of the day, I'm still here, and I am still wishing for death to come like Robin Hood in the night. Giving my soul to one who needs it more, and is more worthy.

All things considered, I am rich. Rich with the scent of death, and with fear, and agony, and hate. I need to get my sister, so that I can finally jump off the damned mountains, and give my soul to somebody that doesn't have one.

* * * * *

I woke up one morning with a thought that startled me. I woke up thinking, 'Why do I slave like this? It wasn't my fault. I need to stop pouting. Feeling sorry for myself doesn't help Zandriah, it doesn't help me, it certainly doesn't do justice to those who fought and died for me. I need to snap out of it!'

I told myself that if I was to get through this alive, I needed to pull myself together. Then I thought of Allen and Irish. I thought about why they left me. I realized that they didn't leave me because of the death; they left me because I had told them to. I had told them from the heart that I didn't want them to get hurt, and that I wanted them to live a life where they control their own fate.

I put it out of my mind, I wasn't going to cry. Right now, it solved nothing. Instead, I pulled myself up high, and told myself that I needed to continue my journey with my head held high.

Chapter 11

I wouldn't run. Not this time. I am not brave. I am not stupid; I am merely stubborn, and mad.

The roar had come from behind me. Then it was the feet. I don't know how I heard the soft pads that held the huge animal that was able to move nearly silent, but I heard it. I didn't know what it was, nor did I care. Although, after a while listening, I could hear not four paws, but eight.

Then, I knew who they were. I put my sword away without a second's hesitation. I was right. I stared into the eyes of my best friends.

"Irish?" I choked. "Allen?"

"Avalon! You have to help us! We are trapped in some rocks! Hurry!" Irish said. I was confused.

"What are you talking about? You are right in front of me!"

"Yes. But this is only a dream. Turn around. We're waiting for you to save us. Help us. We are near the tip of the mountain you just finished climbing." Irish said.

"Forget it! You left me, why would I help you?" I threw the question at her.

"We never left you. We went to hunt, and when we came back, you were gone! We would never leave you! You left us." Allen's eyes screamed at me, but his voice whispered.

I stared at his hurt eyes and whispered back. "I didn't know."

My brain was in overdrive. Was I really dreaming? Is this a trick? Will they forgive me if it is not? If it is, will I die?

"Come to us. Please. I am speaking to you. Dream to dream," Irish said, her eyes pleading, yet as playful as always.

"I'll see if I can help," I said slowly. I didn't want them to know if they were fakes, and I definitely didn't want anyone who is sneaking into my dreams to know that I was coming.

I woke up, crying. I had forgotten my dream, and I didn't know why I was crying, or why I felt like I had to climb up, but something was preventing it.

I shrugged it off; I didn't have time to worry about what my dream was about.

Please turn around, Avalon. Please. We need you to save us. I don't know what made you forget about the dream, but I know you know that something had made you forget it. Irish's voice rang in my head. I turned to see where it was coming from, but there was nothing there.

I trusted the voice, though, and I didn't want to disappoint her, but I had to get to my sister, before it was too late.

Stop trying to contact Avalon, Irish, we both know that if she really cared about us she would've told us that she was definitely going to come find us, not that she might. Now she is just blocking us out. Allen's voice scorched me. Did I really say that I might go get them? I looked back, and saw the two wolves facing each other; they obviously didn't know that I had heard everything that they had said.

I turned around completely and said to their fading bodies, "I am coming, I promise."

I started my journey back up, with Irish and Allen's conversation stuck in my head. Had they really given up? Are they really in the cave, or was it a lie?

I looked up, and saw that it would be awhile until I found out my answer. So I gritted my teeth, and told myself that if it really was a lie, I was ready.

Well, I wasn't all that ready for what was in store for me.

I got to the top of the mountain after two grueling days. It was in these two days that I realized that it never seemed to rain. But it was never too hot. It was always in between. I put it aside, why wouldn't I? It was of no importance to me.

For now, the familiar sing song voice made me drop to my knees, and then it sent me into a deep slumber.

Chapter 12

Burning from the inside out, screams stuck in my throat like dirt in honey. I had to pick at it, and I got a little, but most of my screams were still stuck to the honey, lost forever.

Above me stood the strongest and most terrifyingly handsome creature ever seen. He was about sixteen, with dark brown hair and light green eyes. He was quite tan, and was immensely muscled. The sword he carried was flung high above his head, a battle cry was bellowing in the depths of his eyes, and I knew that I had to spring into action.

I gathered myself up, but before I could spring forward, the sword dropped, and a tear fell on my face. Its presence seemed to beckon the others, for more started to fall. Silent sobs escaped his mouth. He bent over me, and his face held many angry apologies.

He bent down and was a breath away from my lips when I woke with a cry of agony at the dawn. The taste of his breath still lingering on my lips.

I trekked my way up the mountain. Every bone in my body was strained and hurt. The sun had started to come out, and was getting uncomfortably hot for the first time on the journey.

My brain was going through what I would do if I was tricked to come up here, so far I had nothing other than a headache and a hurt body. Going up a mountain was always harder than coming down.

It took all my strength to put one foot in front of the other, to raise my arm and grab onto the rocks above me that were hooked on the huge incline. My only thought after awhile was to get to the cave that I had slept in the night before, the cave that was about three fourths of the way up the mountain.

It had been dark for almost two hours before I finally reached the cave that I was looking for. Well, I think it was the cave that I was looking for, but I couldn't really tell if it was the cave or not.

The next morning was definitely not my favorite one. My bones felt like they had broken in every which way, and my muscles felt like they had shrunk eight sizes and were squishing all my veins and were concentrating on pinching every last nerve in my body.

If I tried to get up, a crushing gust of wind would knock me back down on my already battered body, causing me to twist and turn in the never ending pain in the little cave. I would learn in later years that that cave was called the cave of anguish.

However, at that present time I didn't know that every time you tried to get up, you would be knocked down, and every time you massaged a muscle to loosen it and ease the pain, it would tighten and make the pain indescribably worse, almost as if it was a thousand times worse than a pack of rabid dogs eating you alive. Either way, I tried to get out of the wretched cave, and I kept getting knocked down.

I ended up being able to crawl out of the cave in the late afternoon, and once outside, some of my pain stopped. Even outside the cave, though, I could still feel the throb all over my body from before and after the cave... and from my attempts to get out. Although in pain, I directed all of my energy on catching up with how long it took me that morning to get out of that cave.

It was near night when I finally reached the topmost cave where Ivory and Allen were trapped. What had greeted my senses was welcomed with open arms, yet it was so sad. I could hear on the other side of the barricaded cave the whimper of defeat, and it nearly sent me to tears. The one thing the cave of anguish could never bring is the sadness in the whimpers of those two wolves. I could hear Allen try to comfort Irish, but how could he when he himself had already given up?

I tried to yell to the other side that I was here, that I was coming, but Allen spoke before I could get anything out.

Forget Avalon, Irish, just like she forgot about us. I was fuming now. How dare he? How dare he make me sound like a bad, heartless person? Then he continued, *she's gone, just like her mother. Avalon gave up on us just like her mother gave up on her and her sister. Humans can't be trusted anymore.*

I felt a wave of anger and resentment that didn't belong to me. It coursed through me and my only thought for a second was, why do I deserve to live? I am no good! Then I snapped out of it as a ripple of denial washed over me and Irish's sweet voice overpowered her brother's rough voice, *Avalon can be trusted. I feel her. I know she's close. And I know that you feel her too.*

I smiled at the thought of her being able to sense my presence.

I'm here! What do I have to do to get you out? These boulders are too heavy to pick up. I need some help, but what can I do? I urged to them, trying to block out all my fear, knowing that they might be able to tap into my feelings.

Avalon! I heard the two wolves yell in my head with great joy.

Summon us. Allen advised.

I can do that? I asked astonished

Irish took it from there, *well, sure. You just say 'I summon Allen and Irish to my side on the mountain' and then poof! We are summoned to you, but be careful! Every time you are summoned, everybody who is watching feels it, and knows where you are, so be aware, the mountain will be swarmed with your enemies once you do magic, no doubt. What is worse, anybody who has done magic before can check out who is doing magic at the time, and where that person is.* Irish told me with her excited rambling, as usual.

I swallowed before speaking as clearly as possible, "I summon Irish and Allen to my side on the mountain," nothing happened.

You have to actually try! You have to let the magic consume you; you have to let it flow through you like a raging river. Break the dam, Avalon, break your magical dam. Irish's voice rang in my ears.

I tried again. I cleared my mind as if I was back at home, meditating. I felt a sudden rush of relief and peace. I felt powerful, as I always did whilst meditating. I held onto that feeling, and focused on the task at hand. Then, still concentrating on keeping the powerful feeling, I gritted through my teeth, "I summon Irish and Allen to my side." Nothing happened. "I summon Irish and Allen to my side! I summon… I-Irish and…" I took a deep breath as my concentration broke and pain came back. No!

"I summon my friends to me now!" I demanded. Irish and Allen materialized before me, and I was suddenly knocked to the ground by a paw as big as my aching head. I unsheathed my sword slowly, fatigued by the magic. I held it up in defense against Allen's attack.

Irish was between us in an instant. They glared at each other, and Allen sheathed his claws. I put my sword away, and said to them, quite haughtily, *Now that you are free, you may either chose to come with me, or you may chose to leave. It seems that I am not welcome company in Allen's eyes, and I am not to be trusted.* I turned away from his surprised and guilty face, and started back down the mountain, too tired from saving them to care if the two followed me or not. I was still overwhelmed with the thought that Allen would talk bad about me behind my back, and then attack me after I saved him. It was when he had knocked me on the side of the head that I realized how far down the drop would be if I miss-stepped.

Chapter 13

Irish was right about the whole, 'the mountain will be swarmed with your enemies' theory. Within ten minutes an army had swarmed over the top of the mountain. After about twelve I realized that Irish and Allen had followed me. And, after about thirty, I was panicking.

Create a spell that will get us back into the cave and another one that will cloak us from detection, be specific and end with 'so mote it be'. Irish demanded once we got to the bottom of the mountain, and had nowhere to go.

"I don't know if I can! I am too worn out!" I gasped, frantically looking for any way to escape.

You have to!

"Okay. I'll try" I whispered nervously, my skin sticky with sweat. I thought for a second, and was rewarded with a warning growl from both Irish and Allen.

"C-cloak us from detection," I started, and then realized I didn't know if it should rhyme. I decided to be safe, and continued with, "It has to be p-perfection. For us survive, give us thirty seconds time. Of us, our enemies must not detect, expect, or see, so mote it be." I felt tingly, and knew that I needed to make up the other spell, and fast. As the spell wore on, my enemy was reaching the bottom. Soon they would overwhelm us. I knew I didn't have time to come up with something that rhymed.

"I summon Irish, Allen, and I to the cave buried by boulders, where I had saved them. Transfer us, up the mountain, past the boulders, in the cave. Save us from our enemy, so mote it be." I spluttered, hoping that rhyming wasn't necessary. I felt myself being yanked off the ground. I felt like I was flying, I heard a noise that sounded like a police siren. Then, everything went black. And it was a long time before I woke up.

Avalon? Avalon, wake up. You've been asleep too long. It's time to go. We need to go before we get caught. Irish whispered in my head urgently.

I'm up. How long was I out? I asked through the muddled thoughts in my head.

Too long! We haven't been able to get out of here. I don't know if we will be able to get out without using magic or without tumbling rocks. Both of which will expose us in some way. Allen grumbled.

I can just cloak us and send us to the bottom of the mountain. I told him.

My head felt like it was about to explode, and my body strained for some kind of peace, but I didn't really care. All I cared about was saving my friends and me from the cave, then saving my sister from the treacherous nightmare that she was living in.

I hadn't left her for the whole time that I was out, no matter how much I wanted to leave, I forbade myself.

I had to watch her be tortured, starved, and then thrown into a dungeon without mercy. It gave me a new hate for clichés. I had to sit there and tell her that it would be okay, and that I would be there before I let them kill her. It didn't really help because we both knew that they didn't want to kill her, that they wanted information. Information that she didn't have.

I never felt more at a loss, more helpless and hopeless, and horrified... I've never been more convinced that I was going to do something good.

The grogginess in my head started to clear, leaving me with an overpowering sense to cry. I held all my emotions in, and locked them so far within myself, that I couldn't even feel the huge hole in my heart that never seems to go away, and never seems to get any smaller.

"Cloak us from detection, it has to be perfection. For us to survive, give us thirty seconds time. Of us, our enemies must not detect, expect, or see, so mote it be." The same odd tingly feeling washed over me as I finished the spell.

"Give me a hand, and send Irish, Allen, and me to the bottom of the mountain. Help us leave, so mote it be." I didn't struggle to make up this spell. I had it all planned out, in the back of my mind, ever since right before I passed out on the cold cave floor. It didn't drain me, because there was nothing left to drain but my sadness, and why would it do that...

I could feel myself being ripped off the ground, for the second time in my life, and transported where I wished.

Avalon! Allen's voice rang in my ears, and I knew at once that something had backfired in the spell. I snapped back to reality and pain. My arms started to feel like someone had decided to put me in a huge paper shredder, and then turned on the machine. My legs were a whole different matter. It had felt like somebody had decided that I didn't deserve a fast death, so instead of sneaking a knife across my throat, they let a rabid hyena take refuge on my legs, and the hyena wanted to savor, not just every bite, but every knaw.

I felt myself painfully hit something unusually soft, and when my vision cleared, I realized that I was in some kind of room, with the two wolves sprawled on the floor. There was a curious face staring down at me, and it was then that I realized that my first spell had backfired, not my second.

I tried to get up and groaned, half in excruciating pain, half in hysteric worry that I had got my friends and myself into some serious trouble. I couldn't seem to stop all the images that flashed in my head of my sister being tortured. I also couldn't seem to be able to get through to my mind that I was going to get out of this, the pain in my legs and arms were overpowering any and all sense from my mind.

I still to this day believe that there was a moment that my brain had unhinged, and I had gone temporarily insane beyond any outward help. I also believe that the only reason I snapped out of it was when I heard a raspy voice come from the curious face above me.

Through my deliria I could hear the woman grunt demandingly, "Stop! If you keep up with your attitude, then you'll never be able to save your friends. Or your sister." And I stopped, as if somebody had hit pause on the remote to the movie that was my life.

I knew my eyes were glassy, and showed no emotion. I knew that I had to get a hold of my head, that I had to re-hinge my mind, or everything in my movie-like life would end with a horror picture.

Chapter 14

Allen had a torn leg, Irish had a broken (But somehow fixable,) neck, and I had an unhinged, insane, unstable mind. That too was somehow fixable.

I nodded absently to what the woman who had saved me had said. She had bent down to pick up Irish. When Allen growled at her, he was silenced with a wave of the woman's hand as she finished her task of picking up Irish.

She walked out the door as if she wasn't carrying a thing. A couple minutes later Irish was walking in the room, as if nothing had ever happened, and then she turned to her brother to nuzzle him. I saw the thick black scar that crept across the collar of her neck, exaggerating her white fur.

I choked back a sob, realizing for the first time how much danger I had put them in just trying to rescue them from the mountain. I cursed to myself, knowing that I would have to continue on alone, and kill Bane by myself.

My turn, Allen's pained voice scarred me in a way that nothing else could. The reason why it scarred me was just the fact of knowing that I could've stopped them, and I didn't even try. I decided to give them an invitation to their own personal death beds.

The woman walked over to Allen and fixed his leg right in front of Irish and me. She put her masculine hands over the leg and began to gently, but firmly, pet him.

I could hear the cracking of his bones being reset, and the humming of the woman's power going to work, then it was done, and Allen was able to get up and thank her with a thought in his mind, which she was able to read.

"Your turn." She said turning to me. When she turned around, I made a shocking discovery. She wasn't a woman at all. Long chestnut brown hair came to rest at the shoulders framing a remarkably handsome face, and one that I seemed to remember, but very vaguely. I still couldn't bring back the shadowy memory those pale, pale green eyes.

Going further down, the man's clothes were a tattered brown. No, upon closer inspection I came to find out that the clothes were not a dark brown, but a very dirty white that was caked with dirt and my friends' blood.

His hands looked as soft as silk, yet as rough as sand paper. They looked like they had killed, yet had killed with a caress no other had been able to achieve.

His legs were completely covered with the same dirty cloth, but you could still see the masculine legs underneath the thin cloth. His feet were bare, and, well, with lack of any other word, sexy. You could see every bone, but you could tell that there were muscles in between the skin and bones. He was devoid of any fat whatsoever.

"Your turn" He repeated when I just laid there and stared at him, bathed in my own stupidity. I shook my head in refusal, and he grabbed me by the arms, and sat me upright. "Yes, your turn. Your arms and legs are battered and bruised and ripped to shreds like somebody had sliced and diced with no remorse. I just wish I could've gotten to you before Bane." He said a few short curses as I started to try to get up in the fear that he would hurt me.

He let me try, and I fell to the ground in a river of my own blood. The next part was all red. Red blood, red eyelids… red dreams.

When I woke up the next day it was to a searing pain of brightness to my eyes. I didn't know what to do for a second, I was completely disoriented, completely lost for the first time since I was six years old, and my consciousness was short lived.

* * * * *

I was clutching a small, squealing kitten in my little hands. I was in the pet shop part of the mall. I turned to beg my mom if I could keep the kitten, but when I turned around all I could see was a whole bunch of kids wooing over the same kitten, turning to ask their mom if they could get that kitten that the little girl held.

Then a hand reached down to take the kitten from my hands, I wrenched it back, making the kitten squeal even louder, and I looked up at a mother. But it wasn't my mother. This mother was cold, mean. She bent down and glared at me. I looked back at her, trying to hold back the waterfall of tears that begged to cascade over the cliffs that were my eyes.

"Give me the kitten!" She snapped at me. The dam broke, and the waterfall cascaded, free and beautifully sad.

"N-no." I sobbed at her. I turned and found myself staring at a little boy.

"Hi. I'm Bane." He had said. "That is one mighty fine kitten you have there. May please hold him?" I handed the kitten over, but my eyes were like little scanners, scanning for the most important people in my life. At that moment I didn't care what his name was.

"My parents told me that I was destined to be a great leader one day. My home is just past the mountains in a huge forest called the forest of terror. I don't like the name, but oh well." He had rambled. "It is a huge castle on the inside, but it looks like an old broken down shed that is haunted on the outside." He never seemed to stop talking.

"I know where your mom and sister, Zandriah, are." He tapped on my shoulder, even though he already had my full attention, and he knew it.

"I can show you, but you have to trust me." He had no idea that he just lost my trust with that one sentence.

"No! I don't trust anybody but my mom and my sister, especially not you!" I spat at him, too furious to notice all the astonished gasps and whispers around me as I wiped my tears away, held my head high and proud, and dashed away, in search of my mother.

Half an hour later I found a grown up Zandriah in a dungeon next to my mother's lifeless body.

What seemed like a life time later, I woke up.

I thought of the kitten. Of the little boy that had found my family and I and had convinced my mother to let me have the kitten. I don't know how he did it, but he did. We ended up naming her Cream, because she had such beautifully creamy-tan fur. It was as if she used to be brown, but something mixed the brown with white and made it a beautiful Cream-tan.

Chapter 15

"Ow," I groaned as I opened my eyes for the second time to a searing pain, "Ow, ow, ow!"

"You're up." The man said. "And you sound a little grumpy, and in pain." He chuckled a little under his breath. "You're going to have to get used to it if you're going to continue your journey tomorrow."

All of my pain seemed to vanish on the spot, and I looked around in surprise. "They are hunting?" I asked hopefully.

"No. they left a couple of weeks ago. I told them that I would tell them when sleeping beauty woke up."

"A-a couple o-of w-what?" I was astonished at the words that met my ears. A couple of *weeks*? How long could I have been out?

"Almost a month now," He answered the unasked question with a knowing smile.

"Prove it." I demanded of him, even though I knew he was telling the truth. I remember every day of the month of my unconsciousness.

"You know as well as I that I don't need to prove the fact that you were in a coma for a month. Would've been longer, had I not used magic," his knowing smile faltered for a millisecond, but I was able to catch it, and I had an instant of wonder, but that too, vanished faster than it came.

"You need to stay out of my mind!" I warned him with such ferocity that he stumbled back a couple steps.

"And you need to learn how to control your anger, or else I will burn to ashes."

I shook my head, this man was crazy! Suddenly, I didn't want to be here anymore. This man, this mind reading healer, was definitely not in his right mind.

"Oh I am very much in my right mind, I am just a bit... strange." the last word was said with a wicked grin, and crazed eyes.

"Within life, and within death, hate and love won't arrest, in my time of being, no more of this man may I be seeing, kill him in front of thee, so mote it be!" I turned in time to see the smoke that had permitted the owner of the whisper disappear. And when I turned back, the only occupant of the room were Irish, Allen and me. The man was banned from sight.

When did you get here? I asked them, astonished.

Just now. Who was that woman? Irish asked, while Allen glared at me for a reason that I couldn't fathom.

We need to leave, now. I told Allen and Irish. The look they sent me was one that I knew meant trouble. Defiance.

We've never left a battle before. Never. Irish stated as plain as day.

"I summon Allen Irish and myself to the bottom of the mountain, and keep us from detection." I whispered under my breath to where I hoped that Allen and Irish couldn't hear me. They did. And their heads turned accusingly at me as we were pulled from the ground, and disappeared with what sounded like a police siren coming from nowhere.

What did I tell you, Irish; you can never trust a human. Too bad I can't do magic, or she'd be half way around the world right now. The thought never reached Irish through the confusion of the magical travel, but it reached me. Not only did it reach me, but it assaulted me with its angry words and pointed accusation.

Chapter 16

"Next time, if there is a next time, if I tell you to do something, do it, because the only time that I would tell you to do something, is when there's a damn good reason." I spat at them.

Please don't be mad at us. I don't think I can stand it for much longer. You and Allen need to figure things out... please. The desperation in Irish's voice wasn't even attempted to be hidden, and I knew that she was falling apart.

I knew that, if Allen and I were to part, she would go her separate way too, just so that she didn't feel like she was favoring one over the other, and that tore me apart.

She's right. I sent the thought to Allen. *We need to figure this whole thing out, and fast.*

I was hoping that he would see and hear what I saw and heard from Irish. He didn't.

He shook his head as if his life depended on it. *There is no way that I am ever going to trust you... ever.* His eyes shot out flames of hate that made me think;

Great. Just great.

"We have to get along! We don't have to like or trust each other; we just have to get along!" I screamed to him, and my voice didn't bounce off the mountains like I thought they would, they just fell flat on the ground next to Allen, and scampered back, like a mouse from a cat.

For Irish's sake. I sent to him and him only.

Fine. And that was the only word he spoke to me, and it was the only word that seemed to tear me apart, even though I could never quite gather why.

I turned and realized what I was too distracted before to notice. I wasn't standing in between mountains. The mountains were behind me, and in front of me was a huge tower surrounded by a forest. The Tower looked like it was in its best years ever at the moment. It looked evil and foreboding, yet welcoming. More welcoming than anything I had ever seen before. And that frightened me. It frightened me because I knew that if I were to enter the castle, I would come out in a matchbox, if I ever came out at all. Well, that was the vibe I got from the huge tower, anyway.

I took a step forward, and I was pulled forward twenty feet by ropes that came out of nowhere. Fortunately for me, it rubbed on my sword, snapped, and I was free, running the twenty feet back, and then some.

The ropes fell to the ground, and started to slither across the grass. They rose up like a snake, and struck at me. It almost made the movement look like it meant to stop in mid strike, like it was taunting me. But then it burned up and curled into nothingness.

Avalon, don't try that again. That was a bewitched rope…. And they aren't usually around, because they tend to choke anything that they can get close to. However, they can't go further than fifty feet from their residence, so we need to stay at least fifty feet from the castle, or we might as well write ourselves off as dead. Allen warned me.

"Thanks." I whispered. It didn't take a rocket scientist to see that I was truly grateful that I had gotten away, and was told about the ropes.

I was about to go over a plan with the two when a man appeared right in front of me. He seemed to be in some kind of trouble. He took me by the shirt and yanked me towards him. The wolves let out a frightening warning growl that sounded more like a howl from behind me.

Please, don't let them kill me… don't let them kill me… I did nothing wrong. If you help me, Avalon, I will pledge my loyalty to you forever more! The man's voice was in gasps in my head, and I was too confused to think about what he was talking about. I had only heard my name, and I was freaked out. How did he know about me? And why would he need to pledge loyalty to me?

"You, you haven't seen th-the army yet, h-have y-you? You will see…y-you will s-see the army a-at the edge…." He was drifting off as he said the last word, and his enemy came only seconds after.

My luck was that they appeared within fifty yards of the castle, and the bewitched ropes wouldn't have that.

Chapter 17

One man was lucky enough to be out of the ropes grasp. He started straight for the man that was currently lying, unconscious, on the grass.

"No! You will not hurt him!" I yelled, ripping my sword out of its sheath.

"Stand aside, Hun." The man's milky voice was like a serenade for women. And I almost fell for it.

I swallowed and looked at him right in the face. "No. you are not going to touch him," I glared right into the eyes of a tiger, and the tiger didn't like it.

"I know that you are lying, so give it up!" He purred, a deep rumbling chuckle deep in his stomach, as soon as he saw the hesitation in my eyes.

"No!" I flared. I wouldn't stand for being chuckled at like the child I was not.

"Then I'll come and get him!" He roared. The bones in his body cracked, his teeth grew to consume his face right before his face cracked and snapped to match the teeth. His hands grew larger, his fingers blunter.

Black claws that seemed to never seemed to stop extending like cobras from their hole. His glittering eyes gleamed a harsh blue. And I knew that if I were to get out of this one alive, I would need a lot of help.... Or a miracle. Standing before me was the beast I had once compared the man to.

"I am not afraid of death," I spat at the beast. "I am not afraid to die," I smiled at the questioning look in his eyes. I hadn't lied. Only a coward is afraid of death, and I have had absolutely no time to be a coward.

I thrust my sword up in the air, and the wolves came to my side right before I screamed the ancient battle cry.

Obviously, the beast had never heard a battle cry before, for he stared, startled, for a moment, and by the time he had recovered, the three of us were on top of him.

Irish feinted right, Allen to the left, and I jumped over the beasts head, twisted, and landed on his back like a rider would sit on a bareback horse.

I brought the sword up over my head, and was flung off, my sword nearly stabbing me in the process.

I looked up and saw that the wolves had been flung off also, and they were barely conscious. "no," I whispered. I threw the beast a look of so much hate and disgust that it stopped in its tracks.

You ought to be ashamed! I screamed with my mind, and he backed up a couple steps, like a frightened kitten *You hurt my best friends! I will kill you for what you have done!* I knew that my rage was a bit misplaced, and that I shouldn't be worried about the already recovered wolves, but there was so much hate already in me, I had to do something to get it out.

I wanted to scream, but I found myself incapable of it. I tried to calm down, but the blue flames of hate were licking at my inner body. Then I noticed that it wasn't just in my body. Flames played with my skin, teasing, burning, and I collapsed to my knees.

"You will die." I spat. And at the last word, the cowering beast caught fire, and the shriek of agony reminded me of my mother's last attempt to keep my sister and me safe, and I came to my senses.

"No! You will live, but you will leave this man alone," the shrieking stopped, and the man crouched, shaking, before me. He disappeared with a few mumbled words.

I fell to the ground and dreamed dreams I didn't understand.

Not even the vaguest light, not even the smallest movement, besides my own, the quietest sound, besides mine. Wandering for hours. No obstacles. No bad feelings. No peaceful feelings. No feelings. Miles of empty nothingness. I've walked miles of empty nothingness.

Contemplating, questioning, walking, running. Where am I? What am I doing here? The curiosity in me was gone, but the questions were there.

Then light. Nothing but red and blue and green and orange light. None of the colors started, and none of them ended. They were just there. They were in the same places, consuming the same spots. Yet there still was no curiosity. No wonder. Nothing.

I woke to the bright light of the afternoon sun, and the faces of my best friends. The empty feeling was gone, yet it was still there.

Chapter 18

I got up slowly, not wanting to know where I was, not wanting to remember what I had done. Yet, the memory never seemed to want to just *go away!* I knew that everything was real, and couldn't possibly be a dream, couldn't have been…

No, Avalon, don't go any further! There are bewitched ropes surrounding this tower. They aren't common. They strangle anything that comes within fifty feet of it. Allen warned me. I was getting ready to snap back at him that I knew, that he had already told me that, when the man that had come before appeared.

Please, don't let them kill me… don't let them kill me… I did nothing wrong. If you help me, Avalon, I will pledge my loyalty to you forever more! His familiar voice rang in my head. Something was wrong. I unsheathed my sword, knowing what would come next.

Sure enough, many men appeared within fifty yards of the tower, and were strangled to their death, and, sure enough, one man was clear of the fifty yards.

"Stand aside, Hun." The man's milky voice was as much a serenade this time as last. And I barely controlled the feelings in my stomach.

"Go away, or die." I demanded. He smiled and transformed into the same tiger.

The same confusion reflected in his eyes as I sounded the battle cry. The wolves feinted, and I jumped. I tried the same tactics as last time, but this time I would be ready, and I would control my anger, I would channel it.

I was flung off, and then the wolves were flung off, but the anger never came. I knew that they would be alright. I knew that he hadn't hurt them, so I wasn't angry... yet.

He ran straight at me. I ducked at the last moment, startled by his sudden change of tactics. His claw caught me, and liquid of the purest, darkest red expelled from the wound.

Pain licked at my insides, orange and yellow flames that licked and played at my insides.... as well as my skin.

The tiger stumbled back, frightened, and I said the lethal words that would save me, and my friends, "You will die now."

Orange and yellow flames consumed him, and his scream of agony made me bring it to a stop.

"No, you will live, but you will never bother this man, or any other, your whole life." He muttered a few words, and was gone.

I fell to the same dream, and woke to the same warning from the same wolf.

"Go away, or die." I demanded. He transformed into the same tiger.

The same confusion reflected in his eyes as I sounded the battle cry. The wolves feinted, and I jumped. I tried the same tactics as last time, but this time I would be ready. I was flung off, and then the wolves were flung off.

I ducked right as the tiger jumped over me, and I jumped out of the way before he could hurt me. The tiger landed on his feet, but the wolves attacked him from the same side, bringing him down.

He shook them off as if they were nothing. One swipe brought them both crashing to my feet, dead. I was consumed with the red flames of despair licking and teasing me inside, and out.

Once again, I said the lethal words that would kill the man. This time, when he screamed in agony, I saw his laughter. He was laughing at me, and I knew why. The scream was not his, but my mothers. As if he recorded it, and pushed play.

"You will DIE!" I screamed in fury, pain, and despair. The laughter vanished, and he started to struggle, and let out screams of his own. Red, yellow, orange, and blue flames consumed him. I could feel it drain me, yet I could feel myself being purged of all these emotions.

No longer were they locked away deep inside. Instead, they tore through me freely, letting my emotions heal and letting me vent. I watched as he burned to ash. His ashes laid there, for there were no winds to pick them up, and carry them off.

I walked over to them, and kicked them, my body still aflame. Then I walked over to my now dead friends, and cried out in agony and sorrow too great to express with words.

The man that had pledged loyalty to me walked over to the wolves, and closed their empty eyes. He muttered a couple of words, and their sides started to rise and fall, and their eyes started to flutter, and then closed.

I looked at the man, my relief dousing all the flames that consumed and captured me. "Thank you." I managed, fighting off the sleep that pushed at me.

"Do not fall asleep. If you are able to stay awake for another twenty-four hours, the spell will be broken, and you will be able to continue with your life." The man advised, no longer scared for his life. "I thank you for saving me, and I ask that you allow me to accompany you on your journey, where ever it may lead you."

Great. That's just what I need. An old geezer slowing me down.

"Yeah, sure," I told him, against my better judgment.

"I am more than what meets the eye, I am more than just an old man, I am a healer, of a sort. I can heal all those that have good intentions for others, and who will change the world, or at least help change the world. I can see the future… sort of. I can tell you if somebody is okay, I can tell you how something is probably going to turn out, but my sights have been misleading on occasions. I am, however, positive that the one you worry about is alive, but in severe pain"

"Oh yeah, that's what I wanna hear! That my sister is in freakin' severe pain, did it ever occur to you that I don't want to hear that," my blood boiled with worry, and my heart pumped with the unknown pain my sister is going through.

"You needed to know. Whether you want to admit it or not, you were worried, and you have at least a little piece of mind from the information I have given you," the man's voice was as calm as the waters of an undisturbed lake.

"I hate it when people say they know how I feel, especially when they're wrong," I gritted through my teeth as I glared at him.

"I am sorry you feel that way, but I can help you with your problems. I will be here if you want me to stay here, and if you don't want me here, well, I'm here anyway." His calming voice was starting to bug me as it soothed me.

"You say everything with such calmness now that you are not in fear for your life. What's the matter, you can't take the heat of the battle? If you can't take the heat of battle, get out of the way, you'll be better if you just stay away." I spat. I wanted to be angry, but I was too grateful. He had saved my friends, how can I be mad?

"I will go, I will not trip you up, but if you need anything, I will be here, just yell, or better yet, I'll just keep an eye on you. Be careful, there are many forms of trickery in the world that you have entered," the man was gone before I could stop him. I didn't really want him to go, I just wanted somebody to yell at. The anger at my selfishness lighted my skin with clear fire, the kind that no one wants to have.

"Allen? Irish? A-Are you awake?" I stuttered. I saw Allen's body move in the slightest as his ear cocked back tensely, then relaxed after a minute of silence. "I'm so sorry. I should've known. I should've trusted you guys more, I should've kept you guys close, I shouldn't have pushed you guys away. Can you forgive me?" tears cascaded over my eyelids.

I forgive your understatement. I heard Allen's slurred voice thump in my head, and I wished desperately for some sleep. I walked over to the wolves, and knelt in between them. I put a hand on both their shoulders to start my twenty-four hour vigil.

Two hours passed and my bones ached as the two wolves encouraged me to stay awake. I knew that I had to stay up, and the one month sleep may have helped, but I was still exhausted. We had started to go through the forest after the wolves had woken up. We stopped for the night and all I could think about was blissful sleep.

Quit it! Get your mind off of sleep, if you want, we can start to travel again, but Avalon, if you want to get through the next two hours, you need to take your attention away from sleep. Think battle strategy or something Allen's concerned voice startled me. He sounded so sincere, like he actually meant to help me. I hoped that he actually meant it.

No, it's okay, we can stay here. You and Irish need to sleep,, I hesitated for a second, *Why are you so mad at me?*

I wasn't mad, I just felt betrayed, I didn't mean to seem mad, I just wanted to be able to not trust you...

But why? What have I done so wrong?

Nothing, if anything, you've been more of a family member than our pack ever was, and even more than your mother was... I guess that's why I didn't want to trust you... I was scared that you would leave us forever, I now see that that is impossible because our fates are tied. Allen's sad voice had me thinking. I never realized that he and his precious sister were tied to me by the ropes of fate, but the more I thought of it, the more it made sense.

I never wanted to hurt you, I hope I never do. If you don't mind me asking, though, what happened to your pack?

Humans. They can be very terrible beasts. They killed off our elders and stole our young. They tried to take Irish, but I wouldn't let them. I distracted them while she got away, then I high-tailed it outta there. We found each other a couple days later and introduced ourselves.

Wait I said in confusion. *Isn't she your sister?*

Yes and no. In the following days we became as close as siblings, but no, she is not my biological sister. The reason why we have the same color of coats is because we are from the same region. Our packs lived close together in harmony, but never mated with each other... I miss my pack so much Allen's voice held regrets. He stood up. *I should've done more to save them!* He said in anger, stamping his front paw.

I put my hand on his shoulder, *you were just a cub, and saving Irish was noble and a big feat for a cub as small as you were at the time.*

She wasn't the only one I helped. There were about six others with her. She had told me that they found a cave, and there wasn't enough room for all seven, and she volunteered to leave. She said that she was the second oldest there, and I knew that she wouldn't be able to make it on her own, so I went with her. Allen looked lovingly at the sleeping Irish. He curled up next to her and said *I'm going to get a couple of hours of sleep before the sun rises.*

Chapter 19

The morning sun rose long ago, and night was about to fall again. We had started off as soon as Allen and Irish were awake. My mind and body were so exhausted that I thought about just lying down and falling asleep. I knew, though, that if I did that, the curse upon me would kick into overdrive and take me back…

My mind started to wander as I walked, and I felt like I was about to go to sleep when I felt a sharp pain in my right hand. Allen had bit me. I knew that he had the best intentions of keeping me up, nevertheless, I still glared at the white wolf. Not that he cared. He just kept going on his merry way, pretending nothing had happened. I scowled, the sleeplessness catching up with me, making me cranky.

Has it been 24 hours yet, I asked for about the billionth time in frustration. I was about ready to just drop from exhaustion, and from pain. The bite had broken my skin, and I was bleeding a little.

Just half an hour longer Avalon, just to be safe….I promise. And I am sorry about the bite, I hope it doesn't hurt too much… Allen's voice penetrated my ears jolting me. I hadn't expected an answer, because he had only answered a couple times, and he had seemed only too happy to bite me any chance he could (although this was the first time he had broken skin).

Well it does hurt real bad, and I hope it doesn't get infected or bleed so much that I pass out. I huffed to the guilty looking wolf. I knew that neither was likely to happen, but I was so exhausted and cranky that I felt like I could stew over a slug moving too fast.

I said sorry .his voice pleaded that I forgive him. I knew that I had stepped over the line and that I needed to apologize myself but...

I heard you! I know what you said. I snapped before sighing. *I know you were only trying to help... and I am sorry I am so short with you, but I was already exhausted and at my wits end, and now I get to put the fact that I am bleeding and in pain to boot. I just wish the pain and blood would go away! I forgive you, and thank you for keeping me awake.* No sooner had I said it, my hand started to heal rapidly. I looked down in amazement and ran into Irish because she had stopped in front of me suddenly. There was a moment of confusion as Irish and I tried to straighten up and hide our embarrassment. I soon found out why the wolf had stopped.

We had reached the edge of the forest and there seemed to be what looked like a huge army. I looked around in fright and disappointed confusion. How in the world would we be able to get past so many? There had to be thousands upon thousands, if not a million troops. And not just humans either, oh no! There were dragons, trolls, goblins, animals of all kinds, even unicorns. There were elves, centaurs, Desert Beauties, and giants. There were so many of them! They were all in ranks, and they were all the most terrifying sight I had ever seen. Then it dawned on me....

"You will see at the edge...." I whispered to myself. This was the army the man had talked about! This was *my* army! "All mine..." I muttered in disbelief. I started to walk out of the forest when something had grabbed my shirt.

Avalon are you crazy? There has to be a million troops out there, and about two thousand of them look to be dragons! *And everybody knows that dragons are the most fearsome creatures ever! They are even fiercer than goblins, and there are look to be thousands of them too! I just want to know where they found so many of them! It is also well known that dragons are a dying breed!* Allen seemed genuinely scared of them, and it looked like for a good reason. The dragons were the biggest creatures he had ever seen even bigger than the biggest Desert Beauty!

"It's okay." I told Allen, and I stepped boldly out of the protection of the trees. The rank closest to me looked over and widened their eyes. Some started to whisper to each other. It was a rank of humans. One of them stepped out of the rank and started to blow a horn like instrument, but instead of a loud blaring noise I had expected, the horn made a lovely, haunting tune that made me want to fall asleep. I fought the urge, and the human looked away in disappointment. He unsheathed his sword, and raised it. My eyes grew heavy as my mind screamed at me to unsheathe my own sword. This man was going to kill or capture me. Then I heard a familiar woman's bell like voice.

Go to sleep, Avalon, go to sleep. You needn't stay up anymore. You have stayed up long enough. You deserve to sleep. You have been up long enough.... sleep....sleep....you are safe now with your army... The low haunting voice echoed and faded in my head, repeating itself over and over again, even though I had already fallen asleep.

When I woke up I felt like I had just been punched on every inch of my body. I had no desire to move as I sat dwelling in my expected pain. My muscles seemed to be threatening me that if I move, they would make me regret it. My bones seemed to be demanding an explanation for the unending strain I have caused them... and all I could do is sit there, trying not to move a muscle.

"Avalon. Avalon, wake up. Your sister is waiting for you!" The low haunting voice that I had heard before passing out invaded my thoughts and dreams once again, forcing me awake with its inviting demand. It took me a couple of seconds before I figured out what she had said. I shot straight up in hopes that my sister would be next to me. I looked all around, but there was nobody in the enchanting room.

"Avalon," It said again. "Your sister is waiting for you to rescue her from Bane, you know Bane. Your sister is waiting Avalon...." The haunting voice wouldn't stop reminding me of the name that seemed so familiar, if only I could remember it. I thought I was going to go crazy when, all of a sudden it stopped.

Sis I thought to myself in agony. *I miss you so much and I need to see you and hold you to keep going on. Sis... where are you?*

I told you... Bane...think Bane... The voice repeated 'Bane' until it jogged my memory. The dreams....the...the...and then it happened. I remembered what the desert beauty had said- *"She said that one day, you two would defeat the ultimate power. Of course, that ultimate power is actually a very powerful human. His name is Bane. He towers above everybody, and ordered you, your sister, and your mother killed."*

I got up out of the bed, and tried to stay standing as lightheadedness and pain stole my balance for a couple seconds. The whole journey seemed to slam into my mind at once and the yearn to see my sister to see if she was alright grew stronger.

Allen? Irish? Are you there? We need to go right now. We need to go save my sister. Allen? Irish? I asked in my head as I tried to find them.

We are in cages somewhere Avalon. They say that we are working for the enemy. Help us Avalon, Irish's desperate voice rang in my ears. I raged at the thought that they would lock up my friends. I stormed out of the room and all thoughts of the wolves were driven out of my mind.

I stood before a room bigger than my two story house. It was a completely empty room, but for a cage with two white wolves with nasty scars inside it. I rushed forward to help them and was thrown back to the doorway by a gust of wind. Three more times I tried to run forward to help them, and three more times I was thrown to the doorway.

A voice spoke up from within me. It didn't come from above me, or below me, or around me, but more like a came from me inside me, somehow it seemed like it was me, in some weird way. The voice was strange, almost inhumane, and it made me feel uncomfortable. It said...

It's no use. They work for Bane. Don't you see it, I'm saving you. If it weren't for me you could be dead within the hour. They were just biding their time waiting for you to go to sleep. They are bad. Don't you see it? They were going to kill you when they got their chance...You are just lucky I got there before you fell asleep in their presence.

"You idiot! I've known them for most of the journey! They are my friends! Release them now!" I yelled to the voice. The cage door immediately opened and my friends cautiously stepped out. I ran up to them and hugged both in relief.

"Avalon?" I looked up. There was a petite little girl who was dressed in blood red and had kind red eyes. I nodded. "H-Hi." She smiled shyly and continued. "Avalon, you are needed in the eating room. I will bring you."

"Hi. I seem to be at a loss. You know my name, but, sweet girl, what is yours?" I smiled as she blushed.

"Oh I am nobody, I am just a servant girl, but I am very pleased that you talked to me." She bit her lower lip and looked down at her feet. She had to have been about nine or ten. She was about a foot or two shorter than me.

"Well, just lead the way sweetie." I said and she suppressed a pleased giggle.

"Right this way." She led me out of the big room through an astonishingly regular sized door.

Chapter 20

The eating room and the halls were as grand as every other part of the place I had seen. In the hallways everybody gawked at me as if I was somebody really important. My heartbeat grew rapid with every whisper and every look and every gasp. I looked around nervously, the wolves weaving around and around me as I followed the young girl. I ran my hands over my raggedy clothes. They were covered in dirt and blood.

We entered the eating hall and I saw a huge table filled with a whole bunch of men and women. The most prominent of them all was a woman at the far end of the room, dressed in blood red like the young girl's. She introduced me to everybody with a voice like bells that I recognized instantly as the mysterious voice that gave me weird advice and imprisoned Irish and Allen.

"If you all will excuse Avalon her companions and I, we have a lot to talk about. Thank you." She said after all the cheers that had filled the room when my name was called faded. The rest of the men and women got up, bowed, and walked out in a huge crowd. I estimated about fifty people all in all.

"Hello Avalon, how have you been?' She asked across the long room. She beckoned me to a seat next to her. As I walked she sat down and looked at my 'companions'. "I am sorry for any confusion, but there are two wolves that look exactly like you guys. They even have the same scars as you do. However, they had theirs from birth, and from what I gathered from a man at the meeting today, you have only had yours for about a day. Again, my apologies…" She trailed off, waiting for their names

"Allen and Irish." I told her with an indifferent tone. I decided to be blunt, "I am not sure I like you or not Mrs.…Ms.…?"

"Katanya," She filled in. "I understand why, and I can only hope that you decide that you like me. Until then, let's eat." She smiled at me sweetly as food was brought out. I sat down, leaving a seat in between us. The two wolves sat a little ways off, eyeing their once-captor suspiciously.

Had I not been half starved and living off animal blood, any muddy water I could scavenge, raw bunnies and stale, molding bread for the past month or so, I would've said no thank you. Instead, I ate cautiously, eating what I recognized as cooked elk, fresh white bread, and the best green salad ever. I feasted that night, and drank cool, clean water.

The wolves got a bowl of the same water and raw elk. They feasted as much as I did. Towards the end of my first plate I was given a pill from the sweet servant girl who said it was to clean out my system. Had anybody else given it to me I would've refused, but I took it right then and there to make the girl feel good. I had already decided that I could trust her, if nobody else in this castle.

"So," I said quietly after a while. "I need to know everything, including the date, please."

"Today is Thursday, June seventh. Everything else will take a while to explain, but I will do my best. *After* breakfast."

I sighed but agreed. After breakfast, we went outside so she could show the wolves and I the army that has been training since before my sister and I were born. I thought it was grand and terrifying, the wolves thought it was exceptional. Katanya said that it was a work in progress and nowhere near ready for a fight. She said that they were organized and brave, but a lot of their fighting skills aren't the best.

"Including mine," I said.

"Including yours. And your companions, but that can be fixed easy enough," she looked at me in admiration as she said "You have great natural abilities, we just need to hone them and make them… better. Your companions are the same. I'm impressed."

I felt a swell of pride as she kept talking, but I still wanted to know why I needed it. I opened my mouth to ask when she interrupted.

"I suppose you are going to want to know why you are here and why you are so popular here." She sighed. "It all started when your mother was a little girl...

"When Alana was a little girl her mother and father were killed by Bane's grandparents over two very powerful objects. They were necklaces that your grandparents had made to protect their children. There were two. A boy and a girl named Alana and John. They were two very ordinary kids... for the magical world. They were smart and loved. They were given the necklaces for good luck.

"Banes grandparents were jealous. They wanted one of the necklaces for their soon to be grandchild, Bane. More so, they wanted to combine the two necklaces, and take them both. They sent for Alana's parents.

"Back then Alana's family was poor and Bane's was the high rulers of the whole magical world on all continents and of all the worlds. Alana's parents went to them and refused to make the necklaces one because they knew that if they did, the magic would be wielded wrongly and it would be used to destroy the world.

"Angered, Bane's grandparents declared war...but it never came. Not yet anyway. There has been a foretelling of the day that young Zandriah and Avalon will save the world from the wrath that the grandparents of Bane bestowed upon him."

As the story ended I stood watching the troops in disbelief. So much seemed to crash down on me. It was up to my sister and me to save the world... the universe.

"I know that it is a lot to process, but we are here to help you destroy this evil...you are not alone." Katanya said.

My skin crawled at the knowledge that I was going to have to go against the most powerful man known in history. Not alone, but still single handedly in a way.

Chapter 21

I was escorted to my room and told that the bath was through the door to the right, and my kitchen was through the door on the left.

Wow. My own personal kitchen and bath! I thought to myself.

The little girl tried to give the wolves their own rooms, but after their welcome (even though they understood the circumstances) they decided to stick to me like glue. I asked her if she would allow it, and the girl blushed, and told me that she would have their beds brought in. The girl bowed, and exited through the door behind us.

I went through the door on the right, sure that I smelt bad because I hadn't bathed in so long. The bathroom was even more magnificent than the other rooms. It was huge with a pool-like bath that was easily five to six feet deep and forty feet wide at the smallest length.

I saw hundreds of bubbles and soaps and bath crystals in one gallon clear glass bottles clearly labeled with their scents and benefits lined up on one wall. On another wall were liquids you put in the bath to relax your muscles, or to clean your face, or to detangle your hair. All that you put in the bath. You don't put it in your hair or on your face, you put it *in the water!* The third wall held colorful towels, and washcloths. The fourth had a beautiful painting of the necklaces I wore, but they were on a younger version of my mother and a boy who was undoubtedly the Uncle I never knew. In the middle of them was the door I came through.

I went up to the first wall and picked strawberry bubbles, a white soap bottle labeled *vanilla candle*, and orange citrus bath crystals. I put them next to the bath and went up to the next wall and picked out lavender-mint muscle relaxer, a green liquid labeled *mint face cleanser*, and a bottle of peppermint scented detangler.

I opened all the bottles and put them back down, searching for a spout where the water comes from. I frowned. There wasn't one. I shrugged and decided that I would pour all the scents in, and then I'd find out where to get the water.

I poured in the bubbles first, after that I poured in the soap. I poured the rest in turn. The bath crystals, the muscle relaxer, the face cleanser, and the detangler. I looked down at the mass of colors, they didn't mix well. In fact, they didn't mix at all. I frowned at the beautiful colors and puzzled over the lack of water. I sighed, and took off my clothes, putting them next to the bath. I walked over to the third wall, and grabbed a cobalt blue towel. I put the towel next to my clothes, and remembered feeling something in my pocket earlier. I picked up my pants, and searched the pockets. I found the unknown object and pulled it out of my pocket. It was Zandriah's necklace. I sighed and put it over my head. It hit my necklace soundlessly.

I went to the shallow end of the pool, jumped and let out a squeal of pure delight as water cascaded down from the ceiling and made the liquids separate and made the bubbles explode with life. I walked up to the rapidly spreading water and touched it. I let out another squeal of delight as I found out that the water wasn't cold, or hot, but rather a perfect balance between the two. My squeals seemed to give the water energy, because as I squealed and laughed, the water surged stronger and faster. Within minutes the huge bath filled, and the bubbles rested at just the right amount as I laughed with pure delight. I swam through the bubbly water and felt all the grime and dirt dissolve in the water. With them, my worries seemed to disappear.

Allen, Irish, you should come see this bath! I sent them the wave. Next moment the oversized doggie door I hadn't noticed before opened and Allen walked in, closely followed by Irish.

"Jump in!" I yelled to them when I saw their curiosity, and my voice bounced off the walls. The wolves came up to the water and Allen slowly poked the bubbles. They both jumped when the bubbles popped.

I'm so sorry! It just.... Allen's worried voice made me giggle.

"It's okay, Allen, there are many bubbles and they are allowed to be popped. See?" I clapped my hands and some bubbles made a disappearance act, never to be seen again. They cocked their heads to the left as I giggled. I realized that they haven't seen me so happy and giggly before.

"It's okay to go in, it won't hurt you, I promise." A soft voice spoke from the door. I knew before I saw her that it was the little girl. The wolves sighed in unison. This time, Irish went first. She boldly walked to the edge and jumped in without a splash. The water simply parted and rippled a little bit. I heard her sigh and saw her eyes half close. Allen jumped in, creating a whole new class of splash, and I could've sworn the wolf smiled.

We swam around and got all cleaned off, smiling, giggling, laughing, and having a great time. All our muscles relaxed, and our minds were at temporary peace. We stayed in the water until the water was getting too cold for comfort, and the bubbles were gone. The wolves crawled out first, shook themselves, and walked through the doggie door to give some privacy while I put my dirty clothes back on.

I sighed and got out of the bath, not wanting to put on dirty clothes over my clean skin. I also didn't want to spend forever finger-combing my hair. I picked up my towel, and noticed a note on clothes that weren't mine. I looked around. My clothes weren't to be seen. I smiled as I dried off, and picked up the note.

It read;

Dear Avalon,

I hope you don't mind, but I had your clothes taken and thrown out. They were tattered and past repair. Here are some more fitting clothes for a woman of your status.

Yours truly,
Katanya

I smiled wider and looked down at my new clothes. I picked up a pair of white underwear, a white bra, and a tan tank top the same color of my pale skin. After putting on my undergarments, I picked up a pair of deer hide pants and found out that they were soft inside and out, and a lot more comfortable to wear than they looked. I picked up what seemed to be a white bunny fur shirt that stopped right at the belly button and I was relieved to find that they felt light and easier to move in than my other clothes. Lastly, I picked up a cloak that had sleeves made from an elk. I put it on, and a golden brush fell from it as I adjusted it.

I picked up the brush and ran it through my hair. It was the most beautiful brush ever, and it ran through my hair like the bath water. I brushed my hair and let it fall down my back.

I walked out to the oo's and ah's of Irish, Allen, and the little girl. I smiled brightly, feeling better than I had through the whole ordeal. I stretched and asked the girl what we were to do next.

"Well," She said, finally getting used to being addressed, though still obviously pleased, "Queen Katanya says that you should learn how to use a sword, shield, bow and arrow, and an ax as soon as possible, and the wolves should hone their skills too. She says that you should be able to pick when you start, and which weapon you want to start with, though she does suggest starting with what you know. Do you want to train, or do you think that can wait?" She looked at me, ready to do my bidding.

"You know, I think we should start training." I smiled at her and continued, "And I think I will start with the sword." I went over and picked up my sword.

"This way," She started to lead me out of the door. As she walked she said "Oh and Queen Katanya says that you should always keep a weapon with you no matter what."

We walked out of my room, out of the castle, and into a field where many creatures were learning to fight. A man came and escorted Allen and Irish away with a little protest from them.

I smiled and asked them to go with him. *I'll be okay, and so will you. Go, I'll meet up with you later.* Little did I know 'later' meant 'much later'.

Chapter 22

"This way, no, like this. Slash the sword this way. No, no, no!" My instructor was getting frustrated with me. He kept trying to tell me to slash up, but striking with a downward slash was more comfortable.

"I don't care if it's more comfortable," He sighed and looked at me long and hard, then continued, "drop your sword."

"What? Why?" My confusion was heightening, but I did what he told me to do before he repeated himself.

"Ten push-ups." I looked at him like he was crazy. "Now, Avalon." I rolled my eyes but dropped down to my hands and feet.

"One. Two. Three…" I could feel my left arm protest, "Four… Five…ugh….S-six." I collapsed and looked pitifully up at my instructor.

"Just what I thought. Your arm is hurt." He murmured. I tried to hide my embarrassment. How did he know that? I tried not to show it. His expression changed to anger.

"What in the world were you doing? Trying to act tough no doubt. Well, enough is enough, you need to get that arm checked out. Now."

"I-I'm fine, I promise, it's just a twinge, that's all. I'll get over it." I stammered, eager to learn everything about battle, and not wanting a lame arm to get in the way of training.

"Listen," He turned on me, "If you want to be able to battle, you must be able to use your full strength, so no arguing, understand?"

He seemed satisfied with my nod as he turned back around and marched me to the infirmary.

"Xonia, sweetheart, how has my baby sister been?" My instructor's voice changed from hard and gravely to soft and gravely. His eyes lit up and he seemed to be very proud of his sister.

"I am not a baby!" She laughed, "However, I have been good. What can I do for you bub?"

"Well, you see, this here girl has done something to her arm to weaken it and I have no clue what happened." He smiled and looked at me, "Show her you arm, Allah." He smiled at me now. I felt a pang of sorrow, and held out my right arm. The sorrow came from the memory the nickname sprouted. My sister had called my Allah by the mountains, and I had snapped at her for it.

"Hmm…Interesting…You know what happened, don't you Hun?" I looked away, the new memory of the little cursed town too much to bear. I shook my head, not wanting to know. "Really? What could've happened that made you forget a break this bad? Hmm? Oh, but you didn't, did you?" I looked back at her, trying not to cry as she looked at me with those kind eyes.

"I don't know what you are talking about." I said flatly, with no emotion in my soul or voice. Nothing in my soul but grief and a need for revenge.

"Well, this break was not only set wrong, but a disease was in it for awhile, weakening it permanently. Well, unless you know the right magic to turn it back. Hun," She let go of my arm and cupped my face with both her hands, then continued, "I can't heal this arm until you tell me what happened. It is important that you tell me."

"I-" I hesitated. Could I trust her with something so close to my heart. Could I trust her with a nightmare? "I, uh, broke it…and uh… it was fixed magically" I didn't know how to put it where she could understand and not have me go through a painful memory again.

"It's okay, you can trust us." *us* she had said us, and then I remembered that my instructor was here. As I remembered, he put his hand on my shoulder, silently routing for me.

"I, uh, was at this little town, and I, um, I was rescuing my, my uh, sister and," My voice broke off. I took a deep breath, coughed, and told them everything. How I had gotten to the edge, the fall, the getting up, and the break. "Then I just… kept walking. Later that week, I think it was the next day actually, we took on a bear. When we got back to camp, the Desert Beauties fixed it"

"Well, hunny, that wasn't so bad was it, and look, your arm, and a piece of your heart is fixed." She smiled at me and I felt my heart lighten a little bit. I *did* feel better. Then I thought about how my arm felt better half way through the story, but I kept going because I felt like I needed to.

"Why?" I asked.

"Your arm healed all the big breaks first, when that was done, it healed the smaller breaks. I did nothing really, just a little chant in my head, and poof! Your arm was healing itself as you were healing your soul."

I smiled, and turned to my instructor. "Sir," I said, "May we get back to training now please? I feel great."

"No, you may not!" an indignant voice came from Xonia and she said, "you must rest that arm, and eat, you are skinnier than a starved dog." she frowned. I sighed dramatically.

"Okay." I said over a rumbling tummy. "Where is the little girl that has been assisting me?"

"Oh, Erin? The servant girl? Here, let me ring her." Xonia said. I felt a tinge of anger when she said 'servant girl' but I got over that after Xonia rang the bell and Erin appeared. She curtsied and looked down.

"Hi, sweetie." I grinned as my instructor and his sister gazed at me in disbelieving amazement. I continued as I bent down to be eye level with her, "Would you do me a favor and show me back to my room please?"

"Yes ma'am, this way." she turned and led me out of the room, through many magnificent hallways, and into my room. I sighed in relief as I sank down on the jumbo bed.

"Are you hungry? I could get you something for you if you needed." Erin looked at me with her big red eyes. She had a great want to please.

"No thank you sweetie, I think I can manage. How has your day been?" I asked her eagerly.

"It has been good. Very productive. Here, let me stoke the fire." She walked over to the fireplace in the back of the room. I smiled at her sadly, and wondered if she knew that I meant when I asked her how her day was.

"Sweetie, I meant did you have a happy day?" I asked kindly. She looked at me wide-eyed and I realized that to her a good, happy day was a productive one.

"Oh, certainly, I love serving you, ma'am!" She beamed sincerely. My heart seemed to lift and sink a little at the same time, and I found myself beaming back at her.

She told me that she had to go take care of the foals in the stables. I kept smiling at her as she left, and I found myself in high spirits as I headed for the kitchen and the food that I knew I didn't know how to cook.

I saw the homiest kitchen in the whole world of homey kitchens. It had pots and pans of every size, and spoons, forks, knives, four sinks, eight islands and the warmest, softest wood flooring and counters in the world. I walked up to one of the hundreds of cupboards and threw the doors open.

Inside the cupboards were fresh herbs, loose teas, and spices. My delight deflated as I remembered that I had no idea how to cook. I grumpily picked up a banana from the counter, peeled it, and took an angry bite.

This kitchen had everything a person could ask for... oh wait! There is no chef. I thought bitterly. I looked around and saw some bread. My mind flashed instantly to the weeks and weeks of moldy, disgusting bread and I almost vomited.

I called for Erin and asked her to cook me something up, and she gladly accepted my request. She asked me what I wanted, and I told her to surprise me. She came out half an hour later with mac'n'cheese and a glass of chocolate milk.

"Thank you," I exclaimed, trying to hide the fact that I didn't really like mac'n'cheese. She put it on the table next to the bed and left, smiling and happy that she made me happy.

The mac'n'cheese was creamy white, and didn't look like it had any cheddar cheese in it. I took the first bite and fell in love with the mac'n'cheese. It didn't taste like regular mac'n'cheese, it didn't really taste like mac'n'cheese at all. It had a cinnamony taste to it, and I couldn't taste cheddar cheese at all. It was more of a smoked provolone cheese.

After I ate all the food I crawled into my bed and fell into a deep sleep.

Chapter 23

"Where are they?! Where are the necklaces?" hissed a man that looked as snakelike as he sounded.

"I will never tell you! Never! They are safe, and you shall never get them, neither you nor your precious Bane can break me!" Zandriah sneered. It almost seemed like she sneered more to cover the pain than to shove in the man's face that he will never get the necklaces.

"I'm here Zandriah," I whispered to her. She took a sharp breath and was about to say my name "Don't say my name, they will know who has the necklaces, they will know, so just sit there, and I will be here with you." I put my arms around her and took in all her pain, healing her, and injuring me. Even as I screamed and writhed in pain, I saw that her gashes and bruises were disappearing.

"Not again!" Yelled the guard, looking at her gashes and bruises that were magically disappearing. He had no idea that I was there. In reality, I wasn't there, I was just a live ghost, so to speak. I saw the snake man storm off in a bad temper tantrum.

"Don't leave me, please, Allah! Please don't leave me!" Zandriah's desperate whispers made me want to stay even as...

I woke up crying and missing my sister even more. It took me a couple of seconds to notice that there were many concerned faces looking down at me with fearful concern.

"Are you alright? Avalon, listen to me, answer me! Are you alright?" It was the first time that I had heard Katanya's voice edged with fear. She was always calm and cool. Never like this, but I just stared at her, dazed and numb.

"Move! Everybody move!" Xonia's face appeared in the middle of the others and I looked at them in confusion. I opened my mouth and started talking, but I couldn't hear myself. I panicked and tried to tell them I was alright, then I tried to get them to help me.

"Quit trying to talk, just close your eyes. I am going to heal you. You are bleeding and bruised, and I am going to have to heal you. Just relax. Relax." Xonia looked at me, making me dizzy and tired. My eyelids got heavy, my arms and legs lost the little feeling it had gained, and I fell fast asleep, with my sister yet again.

There was a woman chained to the far wall, sobbing in fear. It wasn't Zandriah. It couldn't be, I just talked to her, we were at home, talking to mom about the fight I had gotten into... oh...yeah, I remember now.

"Zandriah?" I choked, "Are you alright?" All her bruises and gashes were gone and I remembered how I had brought them into myself.

So that is what Xonia meant by I was bleeding and bruised. I had literally absorbed all her injuries. I need to go, sister, I thought, but I'll be back, I promise. She nodded as if she heard me.

When I woke up for the second time that day, I was still in my room, but, thankfully, everybody was gone, even Xonia. I sat up and looked around, everything was as it should be. I yawned, turned over and tried to go back to sleep...

I was flying over a mountain...

"Avalon, hey, Avalon, wake up." Xonia's voice lifted me from my dream, and I woke up reluctantly, my mind trying to hold onto a mountain that had never had time to fully form. Just some blue and white blur as my wings stretched out and the winds accepted my weightless body and hallow bones.

"Avalon! Get up this instant!" Xonia's voice was raising, and I decided that it was best to obey her. Groaning, I flipped over to face her unsmiling, but kind, face. She looked at me with concern and mock anger.

"Grrrrr," I growled, hoping to get my point across with that one syllable. It worked, I knew because she gave me that, 'stop complaining and get up' look. Something that, I have heard, she is very famous for.

I took a moment to consider the pros and cons of just going back to sleep, but the cons were as follows: one; She would wake me back up and two; If she had a chore for me she would make it twice as bad, and the pros were, one; I get more sleep and two; I get up grumpy at a later time. This time the cons outweighed the pros.

"What?" I snapped at her, wishing she had just let me sleep. My bones no longer ached, and my muscles didn't feel all that strained anymore.

"It is time for you to eat and train. I think Katanya wants to teach you herself. Oh, and your companions are waiting for you. Haven't left the room. Now, the servant girl made you some polpeaer sprinkled with fairy dust."

"Made me some what?" I didn't know what it was, but it didn't sound all that good if you ask me.

"Polpeaer sprinkled with fairy dust," she repeated, then continued at my confused look, "Polpeaer is a cross breed between a polar bear, a hawk, and a…oh what do you guys call them… oh yeah, an eagle." she smiled at me as I frowned deeply.

"They sound weird, I see where you get the polar bear and the eagle, but where does the hawk come into the name?" I was wondering out loud.

"We don't know, but we do know that they are awesome creatures, and they are largely overpopulated. They are friendly by nature, but if you make them mad, well let's just say don't make the ones in our army mad." She smiled wearily, obviously thinking about a time when somebody she knew had gotten on the bad side of the polpeaer.

"If we have them in the army, then why do you eat them?"

"Well, you see, there are some wild polpeaer's out there, and there are so many of them that they eat our livestock. We shoot one or two a day, and instead of just letting them rot, we honor them by using not just their fur, but their meat to keep them useful even after death. The polpeaer's here don't care about us eating the wild ones, because they eat the livestock too, and they know that if we didn't shoot the wild beasts, they wouldn't have any food at all."

After the short lesson on polpeaers, I ate, and then went to meet up with Katanya. What we did interested me very much.

* * * * *

"Come and sit down. Don't make a sound, don't fall asleep, and just watch." Katanya said. As much as it interested me, it also bored me. I sat there wondering why I was watching her do yoga.

She reached for the ceiling, then for the floor, all the while going the speed of a racing snail. I yawned and she glared at me. I coughed involuntarily and she would shush me. I sneezed on accident and she scowled at me. I hiccupped and she growled at me.

Finally she snapped; "Dismissed." and stormed out without another word, as if she were mad at me, never once turning back to say anything like 'good job for not speaking' or 'I can hardly wait for our next session, you will be joining me.' Sighing, I exited the ominous, empty, white room and returned to my safe, warm living quarters.

Back in my room I sat on my bed, contemplating if I should go walk around or if I should try to make sense of what happened at my so called 'training'. I decided to try to make sense of what had happened at the training, and came up with nothing. All I could think was that Katanya was paranoid and a bit off her rocker. Maybe I just needed to relax and take a walk…

Chapter 24

"There you are Avalon! Where have you been, everybody has been worried about you!" Erin said with tears in her eyes.

"I am so sorry, I didn't know I just went for a walk that is it, and I didn't know that I had to tell everybody my every move." I said in a sarcastic way, annoyance brimming my voice. Tears started to pour down Erin's cheeks. She looked hurt and unvalued.

"We were just worried, that is all." She whispered, then turned and ran.

"Wait, Erin…Erin, get back here, now!" I yelled, getting mad at myself for my comments and at her for running. She stopped, and turned, an angry young woman had replaced the sweet little girl that I had seen not two minutes ago.

"You are not my mother, do you understand?" She whispered with deadly venom, "I may be just a little servant girl, but I am tired of everybody treating me like crap. Well, I am done, I am going to resign as a lowly servant and go somewhere else."

"What about your mother and father? Don't you care about them?" I asked.

"They are dead to me, they left me here when I was born, and never came back, so no, I don't care about them."

"Please, please don't go." I begged, abandoning pride and begging.

"Why do you care? Huh?" She turned back into a little girl. This time a little girl that was desperate for some attention in her life, somebody to love her. "All I am is your servant, you can get another one."

"I care because I love you. I love you like a big sister or…" I trailed off, not wanting to say 'mother'.

"Like a…mother?" Erin looked at me hopefully, and all I could do was nod as she inched closer. I walked swiftly up to her, and hugged her tight.

"Like a mother" I repeated. She hugged me back, thirsty for the attention that I was giving her. She buried her face into my chest, and sobbed.

"C-can we g-go bac-ck to th-the c-castle?" she sobbed.

"Only if you promise me to stay." I pulled her out to arms length and kneeled, looking at her tearstained face.

"Ok-kay" she nodded.

Back in the castle, Erin went to the queen immediately. Erin told her where she found me, and what I was doing. After that, she went to do her chores, not wanting to disappoint her… *majesty.*

The word stung me, making me think of my father and that awful night when I realized that that woman was his family, and that Zandriah and I were nothing to him.

I shook myself mentally, and headed towards my room, tears running down my cheeks, making me feel weak and pitiful. I angrily wiped them away before anybody could notice. I must be strong. I must be strong for Erin and Katanya, and my sister. Even though she wasn't with me, I must be strong for her, I must find her and be her crutch, her rock, her everything.

As my mind wandered, I didn't notice the tears pouring down my cheeks as I stepped in my room. My mind was so preoccupied that I didn't even notice anybody in the room until I was attacked from behind.

The attacker grabbed me around the throat, and threw me to the ground, snapping my left wrist with a flick of his right wrist. Cringing in pain, I got up, and was instantly rammed in the right shoulder. I felt it dislocate. I rolled to my knees, pushing my shoulder up and over back into place with a crack and a wince, and was rewarded with a kick to the nose. Blood poured out of my nose, giving the white floor a paint job.

Anger and pain overruled my senses, and I forced myself to stand, yelling in pain. Adrenaline kicked in as the man went for a jab to the stomach. I deflected it with a hard slap with my right palm. I threw out my leg in a low kick and felt it jolt when I kicked the attacker in the knee.

Falling to one knee, the man yelled in pain. I cut him off with a mouthful of my fist. I felt the teeth dig into my flesh, and as I pulled my arm back, I saw blood spray out of my fist. I smiled because I felt unstoppable.

Taking my left fist, I crushed his left temple as I broke the right side of his jaw with my right fist. He fell, his kneecap dislocated, four top teeth along with two bottom teeth knocked out, his temple crushed, his jaw broken, and, ultimately, his neck snapped in half.

I smiled, my teeth coated in blood that had come from my nose, my left wrist at a weird angle, broken, my neck bruised, my shoulder throbbing, my right palm sore from deflecting a kick, and my leg screaming from my own kick. I sat down on the floor, exhausted, and now in severe pain because the adrenaline wore off, and shock hasn't settled in yet.

Half a dozen guards poured into the room as I fell over, too weak from the battle to sit up. My eyesight started to blur as the men sounded a call unknown to me. All went black, as I heard Xonia come in, demanding something from the guards. Something about searching and the castle, and the enemy. She probably was saying 'search the castle for the enemy', but I will never know, because I never asked.

"Zandriah!" I screamed. She was all torn up, more like a pile of bones and ripped skin. I ran up to her, knowing that the man hurting her could neither see, nor hear, me.

"I thought you would never come" she said, and I shushed her, not wanting the interrogator to know I was there. I kneeled in front of her, putting my hands on her shoulders, drawing in her sickness. I drew in so much sickness that I was beyond screaming in pain. I couldn't make a sound if I had wanted to, which I did.

I looked down at myself, and noticed that not only was my ghostly self looking more solid as I drew in more sickness, but that the more she looked well, the more I looked sick.

"Ah-ha! So it has been your sister this whole time." *said Bane from behind me. I knew what had happened even before I looked around, then down at my skin. Bane was the interrogator, and he had done something to my sister that would make anybody who healed her visible to him I was as solid as Bane and Zandriah.*

"No..." *I whispered, fearing that I would be trapped in this place forever with my sister.*

"It's okay, you aren't here to stay. After all, you are only here in your dream state. I have figured out what I need to know. You not only heal your sister, but you carry the necklaces that I so desire." *Bane smiled wickedly as he reached for the necklace around my neck.* "However, I can steal the necklaces."

His laugh was the last thing I heard, and his victorious face was the last thing I saw, before I woke up, right before he grabbed the necklaces.

"Oh thank goodness! I thought I had lost you forever! What happened?' Xonia's voice was sharpened with fear and worry.

"What do you mean?" I asked, thoroughly confused. My brain was speeding so fast, I was sure a cop would pull it over and give it a ticket.

"Your body, it just started fading" Xonia looked up quickly. "What happened?" she hissed. I told her everything that had happened, and she sat there, nodding her head and shaking her head at times. When I had finished she took a deep breath and told me I could go as she headed for the door.

"No. No! I will not go until you tell me what happened and why you are so worried. I have healed my sister many times before, and you act like it is a bad thing, I don't get it, she is hurt, and needs my help!" I practically screamed at her.

"You want to know why it is so bad that you did what you did," I nodded. "Fine, I'll tell you. It is bad because every time you heal her, you hurt yourself, and every time you hurt yourself, it is more work for me. What you just did was dangerous because now he might kill your sister. Did it ever occur to you that the only reason your sister is alive is because Bane needed to know where the necklaces are. Now that he knows, you just put your sister's life in danger, and now I have to go to Katanya so she can sound the battle cry, and we can go to war, earlier than we should have. Now we have to not just find Bane's castle, but we have to find it fast. We have no more time, thanks to your negligence. Don't even think about coming, you have made enough trouble as is."

 Xonia fled out of the room as I got out of the hospital bed, still sore from the ordeal. I walked slowly to my room, all the servants glaring at me or snarling at me as I walked by, whereas before they smiled at me and waved at me. News must travel fast.

Chapter 25

As I dropped onto my bed, Erin led four other servants with a whole bunch of armor and swords and shields in their arms into my room. They dropped them on my bed as I got up to greet them. Erin walked up.

"We all heard what happened, and we want to help." Erin said, as one of the servants came up, smiling at me, and made me put my arms out wide. All four of the servants were blonde, with red eyes, and pale skin a little darker than mine.

They started to fit armor on me. They put armor on my chest, my legs, my arms, and steel boots. They didn't, however, give me a helmet. They put a sheath with a sword on my hip, and a huge shield with the shape of the necklaces on the front of it on my shoulder. It took them an hour to finish. Nobody talked as they worked. The four servants left with smiles and thumb-ups.

"What do I need this for, exactly? I'm not allowed to go with them, you know." I sighed, remembering too late what Xonia had said.

"The window is close to the ground, you know. We are on the bottom floor. The stables are not far, and the best buckskin…er… escaped." Erin winked. "Unfortunately, the tack room was locked, so he is ground tied with nothing. There is no saddle, and no bridle."

"Thank you, but what about when they notice I'm gone?" I asked.

"You went walking to cool off your anger, five servants saw you leave, including me." She smiled as I hugged her.

"Thank you so much. I am going walking. See you." I opened the window wide and took out the screen. Crawling through the window, I heard Erin close the door as she left the room. I hit the soft grass, and my armor jingled. The armor felt light and comforting as I walked towards the beautiful buckskin. He was dark brown with a long, thick, creamy white mane and tail. He was easily sixteen hands high, and very regal. I recognized him as Katanya's least favorite horse, Buck. She could never get him to do as she told him. But he loved me. He looked at me with knowing eyes right now. There was no way I was going to be able to get on him without help, I thought.

Need a leg up? Allen's voice came from behind me. Smiling, I turned around.

Yes, please. He came up to me, his sister right behind him. I stepped on his back, noticing that he and Irish both had armor of their own on their backs and heads. I pushed myself off of him, and swung my leg over Buck.

We can go as fast as Buck, so just run. Go straight to the woods. We found out where Zandriah is. Turns out Katanya knew all along, she just didn't want you running off before she thought you were ready Irish said. I smiled, knowing that Erin had told them to listen at doors to find things out, then to come to me. I kicked Buck into a gallop, and the wolves were hot on our heels.

"Where to?" I asked as the wolves stretching their legs effortlessly in front of Buck. They started to slow, and we came to a stop a couple feet later.

We are being-- Allen was cut off by at least a dozen polpeaer bursting through the bushes followed by a dozen trolls, a dozen goblins, animals of all kinds, and a couple dozen unicorns. Among them were about 50 elves on horseback, 60 centaurs, all the Desert Beauties (exactly 100), and 20 giants, along with a couple dragons, landing on the edge of the huge clearing I had just realized we were in. They all crowded the wolves and me.

A beautiful roan unicorn stepped up, *We are here to follow you, and only you, Avalon, Irish, and Allen. The others have lost the real meaning to this battle. The only reason we are training is to protect you and to rescue your sister. We are few compared to Bane's army, but we are enough. My name is Red, and I am the leader of the unicorns.*

"Here's the deal," I said, "Allen and Irish know how to get to Bane's castle, from there our only goal is to get Zandriah out alive, and to protect the necklaces. Then we need to get out and get back to the castle, where we can regroup, and hopefully rejoin the bigger army. Got it?" I looked around as Buck grew restless under me.

The others roared in agreement as I turned and kicked Buck into following Allen and Irish at top speed. The others followed me, the dragons taking flight, and the Desert Beauties turning ghost-like, and running through trees, bushes, and creatures.

We followed Allen and Irish all day and all night, and into the next day, and the next, until four days had gone by of us all running and flying at top speed nonstop. On the fourth night, Allen and Irish slowed, and eventually stopped.

The castle is about a mile away. We should stop and rest for the night. Unicorns don't ever sleep or tire, so they should keep watch. The rest of us, sleep. Allen dropped to the ground after speaking, and fell fast asleep. Irish curled up next to him and was the next to fall asleep. Then, as if somebody had cast a sleeping spell, all the creatures around me, save for the unicorns, dropped to the ground, and fell asleep. Satisfied that all the creatures were doing what they were supposed to do, I put my head on Irish's back, and fell in such a deep sleep, I didn't even dream.

Morning came, and we all were still sleeping. Afternoon came, and we all were still under. Night came, and we were all still blissfully snoozing away the precious time we had left.

Morning the next day came, and the unicorns told us about how they tried to wake us, but we might as well have been dead, so they decided to let us sleep. We all thanked them for their generosity, and then we faced the bigger problem...how in the world would we feed so many? Turns out that the meat eaters got lucky, because a large herd of deer had come by, and the Polpeaers hunted them down while I made a fire to cook my portion of the meat. All the meat eaters got a small meal out of the herd, and all the veggie eaters ate grass.

So, with our stomachs somewhat full, and everybody ready for battle, I mounted Buck, and we made our way through the last little bit of the journey before we came to the castle we were looking for. The beautiful, poorly guarded, castle. I smiled, this was going to be easier than I thought.

Chapter 26

The castle looked inviting and creepy. It was like the line where yin and yang mix. Happy, yet sad. Angry, yet content. Loud, yet quiet. It gave off life, and killed it at the same time. It was the darkest bright light in the galaxy.

We need a plan. How are we going to get in undetected. Irish spoke up, interrupting my thoughts, *they probably have all the doors guarded better than it looks. We need to get in as quietly as possible. What are our assets?*

We have the power to shrink anything we want, an elf came forward with a bag in his hands, indicating to it. *One pinch of this, a few words, and* poof! *it minimizes right in front of our eyes.*

I looked at the elf that had the bag outstretched, *how are we supposed to get back to normal size?* I asked with curiosity.

Well, the thing is, the spell only works for five minutes. You would need to do everything you need to do in those five minutes because you can only use it once every twenty-four hours.

I looked at the elf in disbelief. How would that help? I kicked the dirt in anger and racked my brain for any possible way to get into the castle, find my sister, and get out in five minutes.

It is impossible! There is no way in the world we will be able to all that in five minutes. Impossible! I tried to think of something, but it was in vain, and we were losing all our precious time. I looked at everybody and shook my head. *We need something else. Any other assets?*

Well, we can just storm the castle. There are enough of us. I counted heads last night there are 294 of us, including you, Avalon. A small army, but enough. The idea came from Red, leader of the unicorns.

Everybody thought about it and agreed. We got into three ranks, 98 creatures in each ranks. I got in front of them and took a deep breath, trying to summon up the courage to yell 'charge'. How could one simple word mean so much? I took another deep breath, and decided that the best way to take the enemy by surprise was to not say anything at all, so I thought it.

Charge! I yelled in my head to the other creatures. We all sprinted forward, not daring to go faster than the slowest creature, and not daring to go slower than the fastest beast. We never broke rank, and we were never met by the enemy until we were almost at the castle gate.

The battle began in a storm of confusion and anxiety. We charged forward despite their numbers being twice ours. The ranks on the enemy's side were frightening. They were hideous and they were all humans. Big humans. Half giant humans. Still, we pressed forward, nearing the monstrous beasts and we were gaining speed.

The clash came. Swords flew, shields were knocked down, and bodies fell. Both sides fought to stay alive. We were killing twice as fast as the enemy, but, again, there were twice as many of the enemy than us. I slashed at the half giant in front of me, and cut his throat, and he still came at me. Blindly, I plunged my sword into the beast, and he went down. I had hit his heart.

Go for the heart or behead them! I yelled at my army. Both sides dwindled in numbers rapidly. My army heeded my advice, and we were soon mowing the enemy like grass. I threw down my heavy shield and picked up a sword on the ground. It was light and balanced perfectly. I started taking out two half giants at the same time, spinning, plunging, and ducking. Soon, every last bit of the enemy was sprawled on the ground.

"Too easy" I whispered, knowing there must be something more. I looked at my army, and shouted, "Alright, we need to go, if you are mourning, channel that for the next wave of beasts they throw at us. Avenge your dead friends, destroy the enemy with me. Help me get my sister back, and help your dead friends find justice! Let us break down the castle gates and rage through the halls of the horrendous castle!"

I turned and roared, accompanied by the surviving creatures. One of the Desert Beauties kicked down the gate with ease, and we ran into the castle, all the Desert Beauties and giants staying on the outside to make sure that nobody could come in from the outside but us. The castle seemed so much bigger on the inside.

"Split up! Allen, Irish, with me, Red, split up the rest of the army, leave no survivors for the enemy!" With that, Allen, Irish, and I took a right and sprinted down the hall. *We need to find Zandriah. Now.*

I took a left and looked both ways. *Don't disturb me unless the enemy is coming. Got it?* The wolves nodded and I closed my eyes. I concentrated my every thought on Zandriah. Where was she? I balled my fists, bowed my head, and gave my everything to find Zandriah, and then I fell asleep.

"Your sister is going to come for you soon, Zandriah, and she has no idea that we are on the top of the castle." Bane laughed. "You see? I always win, and once I get Avalon, I can kill you, and take her necklaces. Then, I can command her to marry me, and she will have my kids, and there is nothing you can do about it." Chuckling, he took out a necklace that looked just like mine, and examined it. "You see this? I am going to switch it with her necklace without her knowing, and then I will tell her that the only way for her to keep her precious necklace is to marry me. I will tell her that I will let you go. She will slip you your necklace, and then I will kill you.

"After that, I will put a spell on her to make her think that her army has turned on her." He laughed. "And if you tell her any of this, I will kill her too. Now, let's wait for her to come get us." Bane sat down and stretched his arms behind his head. "She will come through that door, and that will trigger the rope to hang your precious friend that you made down in the dungeon, the cat, and that is when she will turn, and see what she did. She will be too distraught to fight..." I looked closer into the cage, the "cat" was a cheetah the size of a horse.

I woke up from the dream, and I smiled. I signaled for the wolves to follow me, and I ran down the hall, and out the door. Running to the closest Desert Beauty, I asked him to give me a ride, and to help me find my sister on one of the towers. The wolves looked at me concerned, and went to join the battle. The Desert Beauty and I found Bane and Zandriah in less than a minute. He set me down carefully, then went back to battle.

"What the?" Bane looked surprised, and angry. He lunged at me and knocked me to the ground, and towered above me. Fear struck through my heart as he flung a sword high above his head.

Chapter 27

I felt like I was all of a sudden burning from the inside out, my screams stuck in my throat like dirt in honey. I had to pick at it, and I got a little, but most of my screams were still stuck to the honey, lost forever.

Above me stood the strongest and most terrifyingly handsome creature ever seen. He was about sixteen, with dark brown hair and light green eyes. He was quite tan, and was immensely muscled. The sword he carried was flung high above his head, a battle cry was bellowing in the depths of his eyes, and I knew that I had to spring into action.

I gathered myself up, but before I could spring forward, the sword dropped, and a tear fell on my face. It's presence seemed to beckon the others, for more started to fall. silent sobs escaped his mouth. He bent over me, and his face held many angry apologies.

He bent down and was a breath away from my lips when I kicked him hard on the chest, knowing that all he wanted to do was switch the necklaces. I shook off the feeling that this has happened before, and got up.

He yelled, knowing that I had somehow figured out his idea. Lunging for his sword, he cursed. I kicked it out of his reach, picked it up and threw it over the edge of the castle. I cut the rope that connected to a cat that was in a cage.

"No!" Bane yelled and ran at me, murder written in his eyes. I dodged his fist by a hair, and swung my sword at the cage, breaking the lock, and making the door swing wide open. The cheetah in the cage gingerly stepped out of the cage. Once out of the cage, it ran to Zandriah, protecting her from Bane.

Bane lunged at me again, this time connecting his fist with my chest. My back hit the side of the castle wall, and both my swords flung out of my hands. I turned to catch them, but I couldn't reach, and they hit the ground below in seconds.

I felt a hand clasp my arm and Bane spun me around. He held me against him, almost as if all he ever wanted in life was to hold me. I struggled against his grip, and he pressed his lips hard to mine, making me feel sick to my stomach, yet not the kind of sickness I thought I would feel. Whilst I felt it churn with anger and disgust, I also felt it churn with desire. I fought the feeling with everything I had inside me. I took my free arm and hit him in the stomach, knocking him back a few steps. His grip loosened just enough for me to tear free of him. Turning, I reached back and pitched him over the edge.

I ran to my sister, but was cut short by the cheetah. "Let me through damn it! I want to hug my sister!" I screamed at the cheetah, who in turn hissed back.

"Let her through." My sister's soft voice rang out above the oversized cats and my yells. The cat stalked to the side, its ears laid back against its ears. I ran to my sister and gave her the first real hug in a long time.

"Avalon." I pulled back and looked at my sister. Her voice was strained, and her face white. "Look behind you!"

I looked behind me and I saw a hand struggling to bring a body up and over the side of the castle. Another hand flung over the side and gripped the side of the wall. I rushed forward to smash his hands and send him over. I got about halfway when a dark figure jumped over the wall, and landed an inch in front of me.

"Bane," I gritted my teeth. The man just refused to die. He took out a dagger and before I could stop him I felt a sharp blade in my stomach, making me spit up blood and convulse in pain. Falling to my knees, Bane pulled out the dagger. I saw him smile as I fell to darkness.

No. I won't feint. I won't die. I won't lose. My competitive side kicked in and I struggled to my feet as he walked to my sister, going in for the kill. *Get up. Kill him. Save your sister.* My brain wouldn't give me peace, and I knew that the only way to shut it up was to listen to it.

Wincing, I pulled my right foot in front of my left, quickly followed by my right, and so on so forth until I was upon him. I rammed my body weight against him, and fell on top of him. I pushed up on my elbows and tried to roll off of him, but he had landed on his back, and had his hands planted firmly on my hips.

The more I tried to move, the more it hurt, and the more he tightened his grip. In a flurry of not so fluid movement, he flopped my on my back, and he was kneeling over me, putting pressure on the wound he inflicted, making me feel like I was on fire.

"Hurts, doesn't it? I will torture you and kill all your precious friends and family. You will suffer as I have, and then, I will make you my wife, you will have my children, and when I am finished with you--oof!" I felt his hands leave my hips, and saw his body leave the ground as my sister rammed into him.

"Hurry," I growled through my teeth, "Pitch him over the edge... again," Zandriah went for his shoulder, but he grabbed her arm and flipped her on her back. Spluttering, she rolled onto her stomach, and got on her hands and knees, ready to get up and back in the fight, but was hit in between the shoulder blades by bane's fist.

I got up in a rage, the pain in my stomach urging me up. My eyes locked onto Bane. He was the only thing that mattered. Killing him was my whole being. My mind focused on how to exterminate the threat. I shuffled my feet, then started to lift them up little by little as Bane beat my sister black and blue.

"Enough!" I yelled at him. I repeated the word in a whisper, and started towards him. Picking up speed, I slammed my body into him, this time refusing to fall down myself. I went for Bane, and he threw out his legs, catching me off guard and leaving me unable to move. I faded into sleep.

Chapter 28

"Took you long enough to get here, Avalon." I turned around and stared into my mother's eyes. "I was beginning to worry that you would never come, you see, I am not allowed to leave this world without you. I must take you with me if I am to move on. Your time is up."

"I must be dreaming" I started to pace, not able to completely comprehend what she was saying. She took my hand and looked into my eyes.

"You are not dreaming, it is time for you to move on." My mother's voice was a bit deeper than it was when she was alive. I noticed that her eyes were dark, dark green, not the light green that they were. Her build was slightly off too. They were all subtle hints, but they just added up in a not so good way. "Come with me, my sweet."

"My sweet?" that was the last straw, my mom hated that type of talk. She only called Zandriah and me by our names.

"Enough, I am going to wake up, and I am never going with you, do you understand me? You are not my mother, I can tell. So, who are you?" I gritted through my teeth.

"What do you mean?" She laughed, making me feel stupid, "Of course I am not your mother, I am Bane's mother. Now, come!" She yelled in frustration.

"No." I growled, and willed myself awake…

I screamed out in pain. My mind and nerves in a jumble. I felt a sharp pain in my temple. Headache. I opened my eyes and saw Zandriah's empty eyes staring back at me.

"No!" I screamed. I got painfully up on my feet and started towards her.

"Oh no you don't!" Bane roared, and I was knocked back on my butt. I yelled out in pain again. I stood back up, anger and pain controlling my actions, and making me burn inside with so many different colors of fires, they fused and turned black. Black flames licked my skin and healed my wounds.

I felt stronger and surer than ever as I told him "You will die!" his skin was consumed in black flame. His scream tore through the night, making everybody stop what they were doing to listen to the haunting sound.

I lunged for the knife and slashed him across the face, sending him over the edge of the castle, and watched as he fell to the ground and smoldered in smoke.

"Zandriah!" I whispered. I ran over to her, and knelt next to her. "Help! Somebody help!" My screams for help echoed against the forest walls, and my call was heeded. Xonia appeared next to me and started to check me for wounds.

"No, it's her, it's Zandriah. Help…h-help her." I choked. Xonia immediately went for Zandriah, moving her hands up and down her body, and muttering. Slowly, Zandriah's chest started to move up and down, and her eyes shut in slow motion, as if they were too scared to close quickly.

"Is she going to be okay?" I watched Xonia's pale white face stare back at me. "W-what's wrong?"

"Just a little shaken, is all. We have to wake her up, the war is still waging on the castle grounds. Katanya arrived with her troops, but halfway through annihilating the enemy, they seemed to come in droves. The point is, they need a leader, and not one like Katanya, but one like you. A leader who has lived the pain and sorrow." Xonia locked my eyes with hers, and I knew that I should.

"I-I can't do it. I'm not a leader. That is all Katanya…and you…you were the one who said that I had to stay, like you said," I gulped, taking a breath, and pointing at Zandriah to make my point, I finished, "I have created enough trouble" my eyes started to water, and I forced myself to stop…there was no way that I would cry, not now, not after everything that I have gotten through, I am too strong for that now.

"I said that because I knew that you would go, now go be a leader, you can do it, you were born for it; go, before your army all dies." She looked at me, knowing that I was fighting a battle in my head. "Go!"

"Fine, fine, take care of her, you understand? And her friend." I gestured towards the oversized cat.

No, I am going with you, this is my fight too. A surprisingly weak voice pounced in my head.

"Fine, come on." I snapped, and Xonia looked at me questioningly. I shook my head and took off down the tower. I had no clue where I was going on count of the fact that I was given a free lift to the top. The spiral staircase stopped short without any warning around a sharp corner, and the cheetah and I slid down a steep cement hill, and rolled twenty feet at the bottom, both hitting a brick wall.

I sat up, winded, and saw that the cheetah lay beside me, as if it decided to take a quick nap. I shook it, and it woke up, stretched achingly. We stood up together, sore and bruised. I looked around, to my right was an endless hallway, to my left was a door, behind me was the great fall, and in front of us was the painful wall. I thought for a second, and turned the knob to the door.

A wall of blinding ice was before us. People were doing things as if nothing was there…but they weren't moving. I was wondering why nobody had looked over, when I realized that they were in a less blinding ice, but ice nonetheless. I wanted to walk away, to go join the fight, but the room seemed to drag me in, its beauty erasing any other thought away. I pressed my hand against the ice, and was delighted when my hand went right through it, and stayed there as if time was irrelevant. I saw the smiling face of a girl, and smiled back at her. I started to giggle, everything was all right. I laughed a little, a bit more. All of a sudden I was roaring with laughter, and I wasn't the only one. The cheetah was wheezing. Then it stopped, I turned my bright, shining eyes, and saw the delighted cheetahs face shining with glee through the ice.

I smiled, "Good idea." I managed as I started laughing again, this time so hard that I was doubled over, unable to stop. It was hurting my side. It was a stabbing, freezing feel. I didn't care though. I felt *really good.* I didn't care about the cold that was seeping through me, as if I was freezing from the inside out.

Help. Me. The weak voice stirred something in me, making my laughing lessen, along with the cold. *Look at me, stop laughing and look at my eyes...look at the eyes of all the souls in here. Avalon. Help. Us.*

I looked around, startled, and still giggling uncontrollably. I looked into the eyes of the cheetah, its eyes pleading, and very alive. The horror reflecting in its eyes suggested that it was living its worst nightmare. I looked at the little girl, my giggling faint, but still there. Her eyes would be crying if they weren't frozen in her eyes.

"No...No!" I could feel their pain inside me, and I felt helpless. Hate for the man who had captured these souls engulfed me. The blue flames not just encasing me, but encasing the whole room, and I let out a scream of hate and frustration, and as I screamed I felt the flames change to black, pulsing from me, and into the room, melting the ice, and warming the frozen victims little by little. I felt my hate and frustration, and all other horrible feelings subside, leaving me with a content feeling as I collapsed on the floor, weak from my latest splurge.

Thank you. My name is Sapphire. The cheetah panted beside me, and the other victims were all on the floor, so weak that they were unable to wake for now. I looked at Sapphire, and knew that my army still needed me. I didn't know how long we were in there, but I knew that we had to get out of there now.

"Let's go, we need to get to the battle." I growled as I stood up on weak knees. We stalked out of the room, and walked down the hallway, opening doors until we found the doors leading outside. I found strength as I saw the tremendous battle waging on the grounds. An elf ran up to me.

Chapter 29

"My lady," The elf bowed, and proceeded to catch me up on the battle. "We haven't lost many, but they have. However, they keep coming in swarms, and we can't keep fighting them if they have more-" he gurgled as an arrow found its target in his heart. I looked up and saw a creature from the town where my sister had first been kidnapped. I screamed in fury as the clank of metal on metal continued. I tried to summon fire, but I couldn't seem to get quite there, so I unsheathed one of my swords instead. We ran at each other, and I slashed out, slitting his throat, and nearly cutting the unicorn that ran up to me. I looked apologetically, and she swished her tail as if brushing it off. She turned to where her side was to me, an obvious invitation to get on her back. I looked around for a stepping stool, and found a great rock. I stepped on it, and vaulted onto her back.

We will be okay, I just know it. We just need a leader. We need you, Avalon. The unicorn re-voiced Xonia's short speech in those words. I tapped her sides, making her weave in and out of the battle as a response. My mind was set; I had to lead the army. *My* army.

"Okay, okay, okay, okay," I kept repeating to myself, trying to think about strategy, something I knew nothing about. My sword seemed heavy in my right hand, and it seemed to take all my strength to slash it out at the enemy. I looked around, watching the destruction of the two armies from where I sat. I knew that my army had little chance of winning without getting some backup. We certainly weren't going to win if we stayed fighting without regrouping.

"Fall back! Fall back to the trees!" I yelled at the top of my lungs. "Fall back now!" I demanded, and I watched as the two armies came apart as mine listened to my command and fell back to the trees. It was like pulling two different colors of putty away from each other. Going from a muddy red to red and dark brown.

I stopped about a hundred yards from the edge of the trees, followed by my army. I looked behind them, and saw that the enemy was using this time to tend to the weak and wounded. I summoned my courage, and gave a speech to my rundown army.

"I wish we could grab our dead right now." I started out slowly and quietly. Taking a deep breath, I continued louder, "But we can't, and there is nothing we can do about that. However, we need to tend to our wounded." Nobody moved. Nobody was listening, they were too absorbed in their own self pity and pain that they didn't care what I was saying. I sighed.

"Listen!" I shouted above the whimpers and cries. Some looked up reluctantly, others just ignored my feeble demand. I took another deep breath and got angry, flames licking my skin. The flames caught more attention, this time ready to listen, but there was still more creatures not listening than listening. I looked at everybody, the flames growing with my anger. I felt it starting to get out of control and heard myself yell at my army to listen to me. This time everybody was listening to me. The blood roaring in my ears calmed, my anger simmered, and the flames disappeared.

"Now that you are all listening, I would like you guys to start tending to the wounded. Now!" I took a third deep breath, and continued as creatures helped other creatures with their wounds.

"We need to catch them off guard. To do that, we need to split up and surround them. All Polpeaers, trolls, goblins, animals, and unicorns go around to the rear with Allen and Irish. All elves, centaurs, Desert Beauties, giants, and dragons come with me. Elves, if you have lost your horse, find a fallen elf's horse, or a centaur. Anybody who is too wounded or weak to fight, stay here. Understand?" I looked around and thought that everybody would stay, thinking that they couldn't fight, and I hoped that I was wrong. "Is everybody patched up?" The creatures nodded. "Good. Let's go!" I looked up and saw that the enemy was looking around, waiting, but not all that ready.

Chapter 30

We crept through the trees, and waited for a couple seconds, summoning our courage. Then I sent the silent cry of charge through all my army's minds. We charged, catching the enemy off guard. The two armies clashed, and I smiled maliciously as I swung my sword, spilling blood. Within minutes we had the enemy surrounded, and the battle came to a standstill, all our weapons pointing straight at the enemy. They were looking around like pigs, surrounded by starving wolves, knowing that their hunters wouldn't be satisfied until they were all dead.

"N-no survivors!" I saw one of the enemies soldiers yell, with a wavering voice. "K-kill all of th-them!" he attempted, but my enemy just stood there, not daring to move.

"You heard him, no survivors!" I shouted. I looked at the creatures without remorse. We slashed through them, losing a couple more good soldiers at the enemy's last attempt to stay alive. We finished off the last few with victory in our hearts. My army slowly started to grasp that we had won the battle, that we had come to victory after a long battle with a tough enemy. Everybody started to smile, and soon became drunk off of the sweet taste of victory, and the bitter taste of blood in each and every mouth. I stood as creatures started to shake hands, sit down and lay, stretched out on the battle grounds. My smile faltered a bit as I looked back and saw a shadow stumbling through the trees. Something about the shape of the shadow seemed familiar, but I just couldn't put my finger on it. As if it heard my thoughts, the sun peaked out of the clouds and rain, spreading light on brown hair, a tan body, and a man's face that had a long scar across his face. Bane. The sun was hid behind a cloud for a millisecond, not long enough for a man so close to disappear, but when the sun shone bright again, Bane was gone. I convinced myself that the shadow was a deer, and that I had imagined Bane. The sun hid behind a cloud again.

"Alright, men, find our dead, and let's go home," I yelled brightly as I whipped around, swinging my sword up in victory, and swinging it over my head to point the way home. I laughed as my army swung their swords up in unison, yelling incoherently. We gathered up our dead. I turned on the spot and led the victorious army home, yelling and cheering with everybody else, almost able to love every minute of the walk home. However, nobody but me thought about the trouble we might get in when we get back to the castle. We left the castle without permission. We went to battle without orders. Katanya would be mad.

We marched back to the castle grounds in high spirit, and were met by even higher spirits. Xonia had told the worrying Katanya where half her troops were. Then she told her where the wolves and I were. She had taken the news surprisingly well, and had rushed off to begin the preparations for our return. She greeted us as we stepped out the forest.

"Avalon, I am so glad you are okay!" Katanya said as she beckoned me away from the rest of the army. "I didn't know if I should start preparing for a celebration, or for…for…" she couldn't finish her sentence, but I knew all too well what she meant. If I had failed, Katanya would've had to tell her loyal servants to pack up and they would've had to find new land to live on far, far away. "I am just glad that you made it back" Katanya smiled with watery eyes. She sniffed once, wiped the tears away, and finished with, "Let's go celebrate."

"Yeah, let's go." I whispered as she slipped her arm through mine.

The celebration lasted for eight days, each day the soldiers took a couple hours off to go to sleep. We did it cleverly though, some of the army went to sleep while the rest stayed at the party, and then we rotated. But by the time the celebration had ended, everybody was ready for a good long sleep.

When I woke up, everybody was ready for the funerals of the lost loved ones. People came up to me and bowed, and when I entered everybody stopped what they were doing and applauded for a couple seconds, then went back to doing what they were doing before. I smiled at everybody, and waved. I soaked up all the attention, and was happy to see all the happy faces. I was especially happy to see my sister's face. We rarely went anywhere without each other, and Erin, Irish, and Allen were always there with us, sharing precious moments that I cherished and held onto for dear life.

"Avalon, there you are!" Zandriah pulled me out of my thought process as I walked my horse in the training field that was now being used as a place of celebration and horse training. Allen and Irish were with me, keeping me company. Zandriah caught up to me on her brilliant steed, Sapphire. I smiled at her, the over sized cheetah and I have become quite fond of each other.

"Sorry," I replied, unapologetically. Sighing, she looked at me and rolled her eyes. We laughed, and Erin came galloping up on her favorite ride, a pure black unicorn that Erin brushes every day, twice a day, until the unicorn, Goldenstep, shines. She had heard everything, and was laughing along with us. "Hey Erin!" I flashed her a smile.

"Hey, Avalon."

"So," Zandriah stopped laughing and suddenly became serious, "Are you going to tell us what has been eating at you?"

"I don't know what you mean." I looked away from Zandriah and Erin's disbelieving faces. I sighed. "Fine, but you guys are going to think that I am crazy."

"Darling, we already think that you are crazy." Zandriah said and laughed. I huffed out a half-laugh. Allen, Irish, Sapphire, Erin, and Zandriah all looked at me curiously, waiting for an explanation.

"Well, this makes *me* think that I'm crazy." I took a deep breath and stopped my horse. The other two stopped their steeds too. I coughed and said slowly, "In the, uh, woods, after the battle, I thought I saw a, um, shadow, I guess you could call it that. Only, it uh, it was hit by the sunlight for a split second, and it looked like...like..."

Like... Irish prompted.

"It looked a lot like Bane." I finished, and the five of us looked at each other, knowing that what I saw was real, and was probably Bane.

"You do realize that that means Bane can still be out there. Avalon, why didn't you tell us? Have you told Katanya?" Zandriah looked at me, knowing the answers to both.

"Zandriah, we all know that I can't tell Katanya, and neither can you. I didn't tell you because I didn't think it was a good idea before I knew for sure," I kept talking before Zandriah or Erin could interrupt, "I went back to the castle, and I saw a figure on the top of the tower where Bane and I fought. I went into this kind of dream state that I go into, where my dream self can visit anywhere I want to go, and I went that tower. I know what I saw, and I saw Bane."

"So, he's back?" Erin asked.

"Yes, Hun, he is back." I answered, as a tear rolled down her cheek. We all took a deep breath in unison, and let it out as one. Then Erin asked me something that Zandriah and I weren't expecting, and one that I couldn't say 'no' to.

"Avalon, will you adopt me? Please?"

Epilogue

"So, did you ever get him, Mrs. Sarza?" A boy in front of the class asks me. He had bright purple eyes, and hair feathery white, like a bald eagle.

"Well, you'll just have to find out later, won't you?" The old woman chuckled and looked up at the clock on the wall, "Ah, well luckily we had a double period at the end of the day. I must have missed the bell, oh dear." Sure enough, school had ended nearly two hours previously, and the light outside was fading. Luckily, most of her students would have stayed after school much later, and it didn't matter anyway, as they all lived in the same small kingdom. It would take thirty minutes tops for the children to walk to any edge of the kingdom (the school system was placed directly in the middle of the kingdom) and none of the kids lived further than twenty minutes away. Except for the blond haired human, who lived in the woods just outside the boundaries, a good forty minutes away by foot. "All right, class, off you go," Avalon grunted, to feeble protests from the students. The only one who didn't speak at all was the blond haired boy, who looked outside, sighed, and made to stand up. Everybody else was already out the door by the time he made it halfway across the room.

Avalon eyed him cautiously. She knew his mother, knew that she was a gruff, no non-sense, stubborn as a bull woman. Yet, somewhat reasonable...when the mood struck her. The boy was known as Jr, though he never told anybody his real name. Not that Avalon blamed him.

"Jr, come here please," Avalon wheezed, as she scribbled a note on a piece of paper, "I have here a note written to your mother to let her know that you were late on my account, and that I had held the whole class back on accident. I would like you to borrow one of my horses from the stable just outside- don't shake your head 'no' at me boy. Take the note, take a horse. The travel time is cut in half, and you won't be as tired. Off you go, then."

The boy took the note, muttered a thank you with a slight bow, and then shuffled quickly out the door, staring fixedly at the floor. Avalon felt a sort of pang for the boy. Perhaps pity, perhaps a little left over hate for his grandfather. The old woman shook herself mentally.

It's not his fault that he is Bane's grandson, you know. Said an all-too-familiar voice inside Avalon's head. The old woman sighed, and smiled sadly at her companion at the door. Old, creaky, and missing tufts of fur, Allen had a certain battle worn look to him.

I know was all she said. *I'll just be glad when all of this is over.*

Allen nodded his head in understanding. He, too, was tired of this endless battle... the one we call life and the one we all foolishly try to extend beyond our time.

CPSIA information can be obtained
at www.ICGtesting.com
Printed in the USA
LVOW11*0208250418
574767LV00008B/46/P